# CORRUPT IDOL

## POSSESSING VIOLET
### BOOK ONE

## DINAH HARPER

# COPYRIGHT

This is a work of fiction. Names, characters, places, and incidents are either the product of the author's imagination or are used fictitiously, and any resemblance to actual persons, living or dead, business establishments, or locales is purely coincidental.

# CONTENT WARNING

This is an erotic novel that depicts a toxic relationship between step-siblings. This book has been banned from numerous retailers so read at your own discretion.

For a full list of triggers, you can visit my website:

https://www.dinahharper.com/corrupt-idol-content-warning

# CHAPTER 1

"Why didn't you tell me?" Violet whispered.

"We didn't want to worry you."

"Worry me?" She jabbed her finger at the hospital room door. "My stepmom has *cancer,* and you didn't think I should know?"

Dad ran a hand down his face. "We did what we thought was best."

"I don't know how I'm supposed to take this. She... she only has a few weeks left?"

Dad nodded as he sank onto a chair and stared down at his interlocked fingers. "Lynne's tired, Vi."

She hadn't seen her father in two years and in that time, he had aged significantly. The grooves in his face were more pronounced, he had put on weight, and his once gray hair was now snow-white. Taking care of Lynne had clearly taken its toll.

She took the seat beside him and tried to take it all in. She landed in Texas two hours ago, unaware that Lynne had been diagnosed with cancer and was losing the battle, which is why they called her home. She stared at the far wall and shook her head. "I don't know what to say."

"Lynne wants us to spend as much time together as possible before she goes."

"Of course," Violet said, blinking rapidly as her eyes burned with tears.

"That goes for Jesse too."

Her head whipped in his direction. "Jesse?"

Dad held up a hand. "Don't start, Vi."

"I haven't said anything!"

"You don't have to. The few times he's come home, you made excuses why you couldn't visit. Not this time. I don't care what happened between you two. You're going to sort it out, and we're gonna be one big happy family like the good old days."

A cold wave swept over her as memories of the 'good old days' skipped through her mind. Before he turned into a monster, Jesse Sampson was her best friend, protector, hero. And then one day, everything changed. She managed to avoid him for five years. It wasn't nearly long enough.

"Ten years, Vi."

The warble in Dad's voice captured her attention immediately. Her father wasn't an emotional man. He was hard-working, religious, conservative and raised her by himself until Lynne came into the picture. Lynne made their house into a home and filled their lives with light and joy. Lynne had softened her father considerably. Violet had never seen him so happy. Watching him struggle to keep his emotions in check made her heart feel as if it were being shredded.

"I had ten amazing years with her. Next year she was supposed to retire, and we were going to Hawaii for a month before we bought an RV and went on the road." He spread his hands in a gesture that conveyed his helplessness. "We had so many plans and now…"

She gripped his hand and squeezed. "I'm sorry, Dad."

He cleared his throat. "I'm glad you're here, kiddo."

She couldn't stop herself from grumbling, "You should have told me from the beginning."

"It was Lynne's decision to keep this quiet." He patted the back of her hand. "All that doesn't matter now. Whatever time we have left will have to do. You're here. Jesse's coming in. We're gonna enjoy the time we have left."

She hesitated before she asked, "Does he know?"

"Yes, he had to know how serious her condition was to request leave." Dad glanced at his watch. "Can you pick him up?"

She jolted. *"Jesse?"*

He gave her a stern look. "I have to stay with Lynne."

"But—"

"Don't argue. Pick him up and sort out your issues before you bring him here. Lynne doesn't need you two arguing at her bedside." He got to his feet and dropped his keys in her lap. "He's coming in on United. Flight 243, arrives at 4:15."

When she opened her mouth, he leaned down and cupped her chin.

"Please, Violet, I'm having a hard time as it is. I need you to do this for me."

She took in his weary, defeated expression and swallowed her arguments. He saw her acquiescence in her expression and gave her a wan smile.

"That's my girl." Her eyes watered as he pressed a kiss on the top of her head. "It's going to be all right."

When he went into Lynne's hospital room, she didn't move. She sat there with his keys on her lap, pondering how quickly her world flipped upside down. She wasn't prepared for this. *None* of it. This morning, her biggest concern was asking if she could move home and confessing what a mess she'd made of her life in Utah. The moment Dad picked her up, she launched into her speech. She was too deep in her feelings to notice that he was unusually subdued. He didn't ask questions. He said yes before she finished her explanation and didn't give her the lecture she deserved. Before relief could set in, he told her about Lynne, and her already gloomy world darkened considerably.

Slowly, she got to her feet and stood in the doorway of Lynne's hospital room. Dad spoke to a nurse while Lynne lay in bed, a mere shadow of the woman she remembered. Her father nodded as the nurse handed him a list and went over it with him. Protests bubbled up in her throat as everything in her revolted against Dad's simple request.

Lynne let out a moan. Dad and the nurse immediately broke off their conversation.

"Jesse?" Lynne's voice was laced with pain.

Her father's eyes moved to the doorway and speared her. "Violet's picking him up. He should be here soon."

"Oh, that's good," Lynne said hoarsely.

There were things she wanted to say, but like all the other times she felt compelled to speak, nothing left her lips. Six years she had kept a filthy secret locked inside of her and even though she ached to let it out, she knew she couldn't. One utter of the truth would destroy their family. This wasn't the time. She had to acknowledge there would *never* be a right time. She would have to keep it locked inside of her, even if it continued to rot her from the inside out. She had to deal with her inner demons as she always had—alone.

She walked through the busy halls on legs that felt as if

they were made of lead. The sun blasted her the moment she stepped out of the hospital. She slipped on her shades and climbed into her parent's SUV. The stifling heat forced her to roll down the windows. She glanced at the clock and felt her stomach lurch. Jesse would be landing in twenty minutes. Since they lived on the other side of town, she didn't have time to dawdle, but she made no move to put the vehicle in gear. She sat there, staring through the windshield as memories careened into her.

Visiting Texas was bad enough—it brought back everything she strived to forget, and now she had to face *him*. It had been five years since she saw her stepbrother. Even though she made vows to avoid him for the rest of her life, a part of her had known this day would come. She just hadn't expected it to be so soon. The day Jesse left for basic military training was the best day of her life. He was a year older, which allowed her to finish most of her senior year in peace before she moved to Utah to attend college and start over.

Her phone pinged. She glanced at the text and ground her teeth as she put the car in gear. Dad messaged her Jesse's flight info so she couldn't claim she'd forgotten the details. She exited the parking lot and merged onto the freeway. She calculated the time. Jesse would have to wait. Hopefully, he would get impatient and get his own transportation, and she could put off this fucking reunion for another hour or so.

She blasted the radio as she navigated through traffic. She tapped the wheel in time with the beat to convince herself that this was no big deal even though dread lay like a ten-pound weight on her chest. She kept the windows down, even though the wind whipped her hair in her face. She tried to combat her panic by taking in the familiar sights. She had grown up in Austin and after being in the desert, the sight of the rich, green countryside comforted her. The air smelled sweet, or was that just her imagination?

Five years ago, she chose the furthest college from Texas that her parents would allow her to attend, the University of Utah. She moved to Salt Lake City and got the fresh start she needed. After two years of floundering in college, she dropped out and went from shit job to shit job. Nothing lasted long, and she had been living paycheck to paycheck for a while now. She hadn't been too worried until her roommates announced that they were moving out of the house they had been living in for four years. To make matters worse, she had been fired from her latest job for being tardy one too many times. She couldn't afford to live on her own and didn't want to move in with strangers, which left her stranded. She was swimming in debt and had been playing around with the idea of moving home so she could sort out her finances when Dad asked her to visit. She took that as a sign and had been totally unprepared for the news that Lynne had only weeks to live.

Her life had been going downhill for a while now, but this was the cherry on top. Her stepmom, who she loved dearly, had terminal cancer, and she had to face her step-brother after avoiding him like the plague. Life was fucking cruel.

Too soon, she turned into the Austin-Bergstrom International Airport.

Her heart thudded in her ears. If Lynne wasn't dying, she would be on the next fight out of here. This couldn't be happening. The thought of seeing Jesse made her light-headed with panic. This had to be a bad dream.

Her palms began to sweat as she rode the middle lane

and eyed the crowd on the sidewalk. She'd rather pick up a damn stranger than Jesse. Her hands flexed on the wheel as she reminded herself that she was older and more mature. She wasn't the naive teen she'd been, and he couldn't be the fucker she remembered. He had been in the Air Force for five years. The military probably beat the shit out of him, which he deserved. She was freaking out over nothing. They were both here under dire circumstances. Jesse was here for his mom, nothing else. She took a fortifying breath as traffic inched along. She was twenty-three, not seventeen. She could handle this.

At first, she didn't see him and her heart soared as she convinced herself that he had missed his flight or, better yet, Dad was mistaken, and Jesse couldn't come at all. Before she could sail past the pick-up area, she spotted a lone figure at the end of the terminal in a military uniform. Her heart slammed so hard against her ribs, she thought she might be having a heart attack. He was covered head to toe in traditional camouflage. He wore dark sunglasses, combat boots, and had a large pack slung over one shoulder. She was too far away to know for certain, but her body recognized him. Jesse Sampson, her stepbrother, tormentor, and object of her nightmares.

As she cruised toward him, she considered stomping on the gas and telling Dad she hadn't seen him, but Jesse wouldn't play into her lie. He would say she left his ass, which would stress out Dad and Lynne even more. She couldn't do that. She straightened her shoulders and pulled into the next lane as her body broke out in goosebumps. This wouldn't be a replay of the past. She wouldn't let it. He had changed and so had she. This was her opportunity to show him he didn't rule her any longer.

It took every ounce of courage she possessed to pull up

in front of him. She turned her head and felt her insides quiver as he stared at her through the window for a long minute. She caught a glimpse of his smile before he headed to the back of the car. He pulled on the lever and paused, eyeing her through the tinted glass. She swallowed hard as she pressed the unlock button, allowing the devil into her safe place. Her stomach rocked, making her feel ill. He tossed his heavy bag into the trunk and came around to the passenger door. She stared straight ahead as he folded his large frame into the seat.

"Vi."

She didn't acknowledge him. She looked to the left to see if she could merge into traffic and tried to control the fine trembling in her fingers.

"No, hello?" he asked.

She didn't answer. She couldn't. Her mind was a complete blank. The years in between made no difference. The sight of him, the sound of his voice, flooded her with memories.

She slammed her foot on the gas, causing the SUV to buck forward. She gripped the wheel with white knuckles as she navigated out of the airport.

"Want me to drive?"

She shook her head and silently willed him to shut the hell up. She was rattled and desperately trying to find her footing.

"It's been a long time."

She wanted to get back to the hospital as quickly as possible. Unfortunately, rush hour was in full swing, which meant she would have to take back roads that would prolong their time together. Hell.

"You're going to have to talk to me some time," he said.

She planned to show him how little he mattered to her

and how much she had changed, but the moment she saw him, her voice deserted her. He made her feel small, vulnerable, insecure. She thought years on her own would magically fix her, but in his presence, she reverted to her teenage self and hated herself for it.

"Have you seen her?"

The question snapped her out of her inner turmoil. An image of Lynne passed through her mind, wiping away the past and putting her solidly in the present. "Yes."

Her voice was small, but steady, and could be heard over the wind whistling through the cab.

"How does she look?"

Her eyes burned. "Not good."

"How long are you staying?"

Her lips compressed. She didn't want him to know, but Dad would tell him anyway. "I'm moving back."

When she didn't receive a response, she glanced at him and wished she hadn't. He had taken off his cap, revealing slicked back hair that was now in disarray. He was cleanly shaven with a strong jaw, generous lips, and straight nose. She hoped he'd be covered in scars or had his nose broken at some point. No such luck. Unfortunately, he appeared unmarred. He had always been a big guy, but now he was larger than life. He was so broad, his shoulders branched across the console and nearly touched hers.

Her friends had drooled over him. He was a great athlete and particularly talented at football. Many had pegged him as a future NFL player. He shocked everyone by going into the Air Force instead. Lynne begged him not to, but nothing would sway him. He was determined to follow in his late father's footsteps. She counted her lucky stars the day he announced his decision at the dinner table. She hadn't been quick enough to conceal her joy. He made her pay for it later that evening.

"What about college?" he asked.

She returned her attention to the road. "I dropped out."

"Why?"

She was surprised the steering wheel didn't bend under the force she was exerting. She had a death grip on the damn thing. "I couldn't figure out what I wanted to do, and I was wasting time and money."

"And now?"

"I still don't know."

"So, you're moving home."

She nodded and waited for more questions, but he didn't voice any. She should have been grateful that he didn't push, but the silence was worse. The radio was still going, but it didn't cut the tension in the car. They passed cows and horses in pastures as far as the eye could see. She should feel safe and comforted by the familiar scenery. Instead, she felt as if an invisible clock was ticking. Being near him made her feel claustrophobic, as if she could step on a landmine at any second. Minutes passed, and she pressed more heavily on the gas pedal while she diligently searched for cops who liked to hide along this long stretch of highway.

"Pull over."

She whipped her head in his direction. "What?"

"Pull over," he said again.

She stared at him for a heartbeat. She couldn't read his eyes since they were covered by sunglasses, but she didn't need to. His tone had changed and despite the years they had been apart, she knew what he wanted.

"*No.*" When he reached for the wheel, she slapped his hand. "*No,* Jesse."

Her smack didn't deter him. He took hold of the wheel and started to steer her toward the side of the road.

"Stop!" she shrieked.

"Get your foot off the gas before we crash," he rapped out.

"You're going to kill us!"

"You will if you don't do what I say."

"You can't do this to me!" she wailed.

"Fuck," he said through clenched teeth and reached for her leg to lift it off the gas, but she had already done so.

"Jesse..."

He kept one hand on the steering wheel while the other went to her neck and massaged the tense muscles. "Good girl."

"Don't," she seethed.

"Shh. Turn here. Come on, you know where to go."

She was so rattled she could barely think. "T-think about Mom. We have to—"

"I'll see her after I see to you."

He had taken her down many deserted roads during her junior year of high school. They spent more time than she cared to remember at every rest stop or park along the way to their house.

She dragged his hand from her neck and thrust it away from her as she stopped under the shade of a familiar tree. "You can't—"

Two large hands gripped her face and hauled her over the console, dislodging her shades. His lips covered hers and when she tried to scream, his tongue thrust in, and she choked on it. Her body flushed with biting cold and then a searing heat that felt as if she was being nipped by thousands of fire ants. She gripped handfuls of his hair and tried to yank his head back, but it had no effect on him whatsoever. One hand clasped her nape to keep her still while the other quested down her body. He gripped her breast through her thin shirt. She bucked and raked her nails down his cheek.

When he reared back, she felt a burst of relief until he unsnapped her seat belt.

"Jesse, you can't do this anymore!"

His response was to drag her out of her seat and onto his lap. She let out an enraged bellow and slapped him, knocking his glasses off his face to reveal sky-blue eyes clouded with lust and fury. If she'd seen his eyes when she pulled up to the curb, she never would have let him in the car.

"Jesse," she whispered, but he ignored her and shoved his door open.

She looked around as he stepped out with her in his arms. When she was younger, she'd been too ashamed to ask for help, but times had changed. This time, she was desperate enough to get someone's attention, but there was no one in the empty parking lot to come to her rescue. If she had known he would revert to old habits, she would have taken a different route.

"Jesse, you can't—"

He ignored her struggles as he opened the back door, folded the back seats by pulling on a lever, and tossed her in.

She lunged between the front seats to get to her phone, but he pushed her aside as he climbed in, using his body to force her into the trunk. She knew from experience there was no way to open the back door from the inside. Her mind glazed with nightmares as he boxed her in.

"Five years," he bit out as he crawled toward where she huddled in the furthest corner.

She held her hands up to ward him off. "Jesse, you can't do this. It's rape! You have no *right*—"

Her voice was cut off as he grabbed her and swung her to the floor. He shoved his pack to the side as he crouched over her.

"Rape?"

His voice was curiously soft as he hovered over her like a massive lion. His eyes moved over her as his hand splayed over her quivering stomach.

"You want me, you just won't admit it."

She levered herself up to get in his face. "I *don't* want you! I never did! You forced me!"

He eased closer, so their lips were a breath apart. "You want me to fight you for it."

"You conceited mother*fuck*—"

His mouth collided with hers. When she dropped to disengage their lips, a hand cradled the back of her head to keep her in place. When he moaned, her nipples grew hard. She clawed him, but his uniform protected him from harm. His hand went between them and undid her shorts. She bucked and fought, but he yanked them down with brute force.

"Stop!" she sobbed.

"No fucking way."

He tossed her shorts and underwear and grabbed her shirt. When it ripped, she hit him again, which caused him to pin her arms over her head. He leaned down and bit her breast.

"Behave," he said around her nipple.

"I hate you!"

He moved to the other breast and sucked until she screamed and pleaded for him to stop. He gentled and flicked her nipple with his tongue. She stared at the ceiling and prayed this was a nightmare, but the feel of his coarse uniform brushing over her bare skin was too fucking real to be a figment of her imagination. This was happening and there was nothing she could do to stop it.

He dragged her shirt off and then balled it beneath her head as a makeshift pillow. He forced her legs apart and slid a finger inside her. Her body bowed and her toes curled. She gripped his wrist.

"Please stop."

"You know I can't."

Eyes wet with tears met his fevered ones. "You mean you won't."

He focused on his hand moving between her thighs. "No, I can't. This..." He shook his head and gripped his dick through his uniform and began to stroke. "I can't help myself. You're wet, but it's not enough. What do you need?"

"I need you to leave me alone!"

"Not gonna happen."

He scooted her up so he could stretch out on his belly. She tried to roll away, but he spread her legs and put his mouth on her. She screamed. He lifted her thighs as he stabbed deep. She tried to suffocate him, but his groans told her he was far from dead. No matter how hard she fought, she couldn't win. She tried to ignore his caresses as he played her body, but he knew what got her off. It didn't take long for him to make her come.

When she lay limp and defeated beneath him, he lifted his face, which was smeared with her. He jerked her under him and fumbled with his pants as he settled between her quaking thighs. He kissed her, forcing her to taste herself as he slid inside her. He shuddered and broke the kiss to pant, "Fuck!"

She felt as if she was floating out of her body as her

pussy yielded to him. He yanked on her hair until she looked at him.

"You know how long I've been waiting for this?" He pulled out and then slipped back in. "You know how many times I've jacked off, imagining you beneath me, smelling your hair, having you look at me..." He quivered above her. The tendons in his neck stood out as he struggled for control. "Fuck, I can't wait. I need you."

That was the only warning he got before he fucked her. No finesse, no technique, just animal lust. He pounded her into the hard floor and within minutes, climaxed. She got rug burn and bruises in the process, but she didn't make a sound. When it was over, he braced himself over her, his hot breath fanning her face. Slowly, he pulled out of her. She followed his gaze and watched him drip over her. He had a thing for his cum. Sure enough, his hand played with his semen in her pussy before he smoothed it over her stomach. His eyes bored into hers as he leaned down and kissed her. This time, she didn't fight it.

"No more running, Vi."

# CHAPTER 2

Violet stayed in the trunk since he destroyed her shirt. She wasn't about to sit in the passenger seat in her bra. She tipped from side to side as he finished the drive home. Her pussy throbbed, and her senses were elevated, while her spirit was heavy. It happened again. Five years didn't mean shit. He hadn't changed and neither had she since she'd just been thoroughly fucked.

She didn't move when he parked. When the garage door came down, they were encased in darkness. The interior light came on as he stepped out of the car. She told herself to grab her shorts and bolt before he could do anything else, but she lay there like a dead thing. The trunk door rose. She sensed him standing there, examining her. He reached in and shouldered his bag before he grabbed her ankle and dragged her toward him.

"Ow!" she snapped and tried to kick him.

He pinned her ass on the tailgate and kissed her pussy before he hauled her into his arms. He managed to grab her ruined shirt and shorts and juggled them all as he carried her into the house.

"Let me go!" she hissed as she tried to get free.

"In a minute."

He walked into his bedroom and dropped his pack on the floor before he walked into their Jack and Jill bathroom.

"We aren't showering together!" she spat.

He set her in the tub and eyed her as he dropped her ruined clothes on the floor and stripped off his uniform. Her mouth went dry as she took him in. When she was seventeen, he forced her to learn every inch of his body. His years in the military had changed his physique beyond recognition. Every inch of him was solid muscle. She held up her hands as he stepped in with her.

"Please don't," she whispered.

"I'm not going to hurt you."

She punched him in the stomach. "Then what was that in the car? You hurt me all the time! No matter how many times I beg you to stop, you *never*—"

He kissed her, putting a stop to her escalating voice and emotions. He picked her up and pressed her against the wall. His last load helped ease his entry this time. He fucked her nice and slow, the enclosed space amplifying the sound of her panting and hitched breaths. He covered her face with kisses and when he came again, he whispered, "There's no one like you."

"I hate you."

He bathed her, blocking any escape with his big body. He detached the shower nozzle to clean his cum from her and asked casually, "Are you on anything?"

She went rigid. "What?"

His eyes were steady on hers, eyelashes spiked with water as he waited for an answer. She renewed her struggles to get away from him.

"I'm... I'm..." Her mind was blank with fear.

"You aren't on anything?"

"I-I didn't pick up my pills after I broke up with my last boyfriend."

His eyes darkened. "What the fuck did you say?"

"Jesse."

He gripped her face. "You know how I feel about you with other guys."

"You don't own me."

"You think not?"

Two fingers slid into her pussy. He pinned her against the wet tiles as his hand worked her. She was swollen and throbbing and when he scraped his fingers against her G spot, she nearly brained herself when her head kicked back.

"You know what I did to Tucker. We don't want any more accidents, do we?"

She clawed his arm. "Jesse, *stop!*"

He applied pressure, making her cramp. She screamed and gripped his wrist with both hands, trying to pull those marauding, brutal fingers out of her. A hand wrapped around her throat and squeezed, forcing her eyes to his. He pressed his wet forehead against hers.

"Tell me how many you've been with, so I know how to punish you."

"Fuck you!"

He did something that made her womb weep. She hunched over as he kissed her temple.

"Tell me," he ordered.

She glared at him. "Too many to count," she panted with relish.

He wrenched her head back and kissed her hard. "You're gonna regret that."

He finished washing her before allowing her to stumble out of the shower. She wrapped herself in a fluffy towel and fled to her room where she locked both doors—the one that connected to the bathroom and the other that led into the hallway. She stood in the middle of the room, mind awhirl with fragmented thoughts. She couldn't stay here, not with Jesse around. It didn't take more than thirty minutes for him to get her on her back. He wouldn't stop. She knew that from experience. He would take what he wanted anytime, anywhere and leave her wasted and empty again. She clamped her trembling thighs together. She would tell Dad and Lynne that she had to go back to Utah to pack up her life there. Hopefully, by the time she came back, Jesse's leave would be up, and she could focus on Mom without that fucker ruining everything.

She dropped to her knees beside her open suitcase and pulled on jeans and a new top. She stood in front of the floor length mirror and brushed her hair while her mind buzzed with static. Her reflection had changed little in the intervening years and the fact that her bedroom remained untouched gave her an odd sense of déjà vu. The hydrangea bedspread was the same, as were the matching curtains. Everything was bright and colorful, but it was a sham. Unspeakable depravity clung to the walls of this place. The few times she came home for a visit, she slept on the couch. Dad thought this was a weird quirk of hers. He didn't realize that she couldn't be in this room without remembering the hell Jesse put her through. Seeing that soft cotton candy shade of blue or pink sent her spiraling into the past. She nixed those colors from her life and preferred black and gray instead.

She pressed her ear against the door that led into the bathroom. No sound. Cautiously, she unlocked it and found the bathroom empty. The door leading to his room was open. Quick and silent, she swung it closed and didn't breathe until it was locked. She kicked her shorts and ripped shirt into the corner and pulled out the blow-dryer. When she flipped it on, her eyes went to his door. She expected him to try to break the door down or shout at her, but nothing happened.

She did her best to dry her wavy, long black hair as her hands shook. She focused on her task and refused to dwell on what happened. She would blank it from her mind, as she had done all the other incidents. Her goal was to get back to the hospital where their parents were. There was safety in numbers. She would bring Dad home and then escape back to Utah, where she would bide her time until Jesse left.

Her hazel eyes looked green in the bright light. People often mentioned her eyes changed color with her moods. She hadn't seen her eyes this particular shade in years. Her lips were a little swollen and her body was throbbing, but nothing showed on the surface. He had always been careful not to mark her too much. She shuddered.

When she walked into her bedroom, she stopped short when she found Jesse sitting on her bed. Her eyes flicked to the door she had locked before she met his inscrutable gaze.

"Ready?" he asked.

He was going to act like nothing happened. Of course, he was. His moods were as quick-changing as the Texas weather. As a teen, his abrupt personality switches gave her whiplash. He was so good at playing a role while she floundered and struggled to conceal her emotions. Five years later, nothing had changed. Jesse taught her a lot about men. Men only wanted one thing, and once they got it, she ceased to exist for them. She tried to go lesbian even though she knew it would give her religious father a heart attack, but unfortunately, women didn't do anything for her sexually. She indulged in a long string of lovers that didn't add up to much and only reinforced the fact that most men sucked.

"Ready." She was proud her voice sounded even and cool when she felt as sturdy as tissue paper.

He got to his feet, and she noticed for the first time that he was in jeans and a white shirt. His casual attire reminded her so much of the past that she went dizzy for a moment.

"Vi?"

She shook herself and marched toward the door. "Let's go."

She led the way to the garage and hesitated before she slipped into the front passenger seat. Sitting in the back would only start an argument, and she didn't want to give him a reason to put his hands on her again. Now that he got what he wanted, he would behave for a while. She had to keep him on an even keel. All she had to do was sit here until they made it to the hospital. She could handle that, right?

He slipped into the driver's side. When he backed out of the garage, he turned toward her and draped his arm around the back of her seat. She shied away from him. He caught the small movement and stared at her for a few beats before he put the car in drive.

She leaned against the window and examined the neighborhood, which hadn't changed much. A neighbor recognized the car and waved. Out of the corner of her eye, she saw Jesse lift his hand in acknowledgment. Jesse, the golden boy with impeccable manners. No one would believe what had been going on under everyone's noses for years.

She clamped her legs together as her pussy pulsed. She climaxed. What the fuck? He turned her body against her, as he had when they were teens. How she felt about him didn't matter. He could manipulate her body and took great pleasure in doing so. Once, she had loved him with every fiber of her being, but things started to change when she turned sixteen. She woke several times in the middle of the night to find him in her room. At the time, she refused to believe what was happening and came up with a ton of excuses for him, but when she was seventeen, they hit the point of no return. The veil of denial was ripped to shreds when he fucked her. And when it continued, she had no choice but to conclude the stepbrother she had once idolized was a depraved psychopath. The strain of pretending that everything was normal while Jesse forced her compliance broke her. Her threats, hate, or silence made no impact on him. He stole everything from her... and he was still doing it. He was heartless.

She pictured their reunion many times over the years. In some fantasies, she kneed him in the balls. In others, she smacked him across the face and in her favorite, she was able to skewer him with a look, and he fell to his knees and begged for forgiveness. Her insides writhed with shame. None of those came true. She put up a fight, but it didn't matter. He still won. He *always* won.

Neither of them said a word during the ride. The moment he parked, she was out the door. Although she hurried ahead, he easily caught up with her. She was five foot six, but Jesse was a freaking giant at six foot three. As they entered the hospital, her mind switched from her issues with Jesse to the larger one—Lynne's impending death.

She glanced at him as he paced beside her. He looked

unruffled, relaxed, and unaffected by his surroundings. How could he be so calm when his mom had only weeks to live? Wasn't he terrified? Dreading the end? If he felt anything, it didn't show on the surface.

Sensing her regard, he turned his head and speared her with those eyes that haunted her dreams. She looked away and noticed he was attracting quite a bit of attention. That was no surprise. Women had been throwing themselves at him for as long as she had known him. He never lacked female attention, so why had he fixated on her? Why risk so much to fuck his stepsister? Was it because it was taboo? Because she was the only female who didn't want him? Or was she just convenient and he enjoyed controlling her? Whatever his reasons, he was a sick bastard.

The door to Lynne's room was open, so she walked in with Jesse following in her wake. Dad sat beside the bed with Lynne's hand pressed against his mouth as they talked. Her heart clenched when Dad turned his head, revealing glistening eyes. He looked down to compose himself as Jesse rounded the bed to greet his mother.

"Jesse, you're home!" Lynne cried.

Violet went to her father's side. "Dad, are you okay?"

"I'm good," he said with a pained smile.

He clearly wasn't, but she didn't want to embarrass him further, so she switched her attention to the mother and son reunion taking place. Lynne looked even smaller in comparison to her son's bulky frame. Jesse reached out and cupped his mother's face. Something twisted in Violet's stomach as they smiled at one another. Lynne stared at Jesse with luminous eyes. It was clear she adored her son, and it wasn't one-sided. Jesse pressed his forehead against his mother's and whispered to her as tears trickled down her cheek.

"I'm so happy you're here," Lynne said.

"Nowhere else I'd rather be," Jesse murmured.

Violet turned away and pressed a hand against her mouth as her stomach rocked with nausea. How could he be the monster who forced himself on her and the loving, doting son not even twenty minutes later? He was doing it again—making her doubt her sanity by transitioning seamlessly between his multiple personalities.

"What are these marks on your cheek?" Lynne asked.

Violet stopped breathing.

"I was helping a woman get her luggage from the overhead bin and a buckle scratched my face," Jesse answered.

Violet swiped at the cold sweat on her brow. He said it so easily, so effortlessly. She would have believed him if she hadn't put the scratches there herself. How did he lie so effortlessly?

"I'm so glad you're here, son," Dad said.

She heard the manly clap on the back they gave each other and then Jesse's, "It's good to be home."

Her father loved Jesse. He had no reason not to. Jesse was well-liked by their parents and everyone in the community. To everyone else he was well-mannered, courteous, and a hard worker. No one would dream that there was something wrong with him. It was only when she and Jesse were alone that he morphed into an entirely different person.

She listened, dumbfounded, as Jesse talked to her father about fishing. He was so composed, so damn smooth, she wanted to pull her hair out. She didn't know what to say or how to act. He made her feel isolated, lonely, bereft. The only way she knew how to cope was to ignore Jesse and stuff her emotions into the dark corners until she was alone. She had been in Austin for only a few hours and was already on the brink of a breakdown.

"Vi."

She turned to see Lynne holding out her hand. She ignored the men and went to her mother's side. Lynne wore a pretty silk scarf wrapped around her bald head. She had thinned and was alarmingly pale, but her smile never wavered. Lynne grasped her hand in a surprisingly firm grip.

"I'm so happy to see you two together," Lynne gushed. "You had time to talk and settle your differences?"

Dad and Jesse were on the other side of the bed. They were talking, but Jesse was turned toward her. She could feel his gaze on her. Was he worried she would tell the truth? There was a tiny voice in the back of her mind that urged her to spill, but she wouldn't, and he knew it. Lynne was waiting for an answer. She looked so goddamn hopeful that Violet didn't have the heart to disappoint her. She nodded because she couldn't speak.

"I'm so glad." Lynne kissed the back of her hand. "You two used to be so close. Once Dad and I are gone, you're all each other has."

"Stop talking like that. I can't..." Violet shook her head as her throat closed.

"I'm sorry I kept this from you. I know you've had your struggles in Utah. I didn't want to add to that."

"But..." Violet's eyes filled with tears. "I wish I'd known. I could have been here for you."

Lynne cupped her cheek with an ice-cold hand. "My sweet girl. This isn't something you should be around. It's been a long journey of tests, bad news, and dashed hopes. You have your whole life ahead of you. If I told you, you would be as tired as your father. This way, you're focused on the here and now. We know the verdict and we have time. That's all that matters."

Violet brushed away a tear. "What happens now?"

"I'm coming home tomorrow."

She stiffened. "You're refusing treatment?"

"There's nothing more they can do, and I want to be home."

"But what if—"

"It's all set, Vi."

"This can't be all they can do for you!"

"It is." Lynne's smile stretched even wider as a tear slid down her cheek. "We've done everything possible, but it wasn't good enough. My time's up, but I have some requests before I kick the bucket."

"Mom!"

Lynne slumped against the pillows and laughed. Violet didn't know how to handle Lynne's cavalier attitude about her mortality. She had never found anything less humorous in her life. When Lynne saw her expression, she sobered.

"I'm sorry, honey. I know this is hitting you all at once, but dying is a part of life. We're not promised tomorrow. At least you know I'm about to die instead of getting a phone call from Dad saying I was killed in a car accident or something."

True, but *still*. "I'm... I can't think right now."

"Both of you must be exhausted. You should get some rest. Dad and I will be home tomorrow."

Alarm bells went off in her mind. She looked at Dad as he rounded the bed. "You aren't coming home?"

"No, I'm spending the night here with Mom."

Violet's gaze flicked to Jesse. "Maybe I should stay, too."

"Absolutely not," Lynne said firmly. "Staying in hospitals isn't fun. You two go out to dinner. Isaac, give them some money."

When Dad reached into his pocket, Jesse shook his head.

"We're good. I have money."

"So, do I," Violet said, even though she'd have to charge a meal to her credit card.

Lynne waved her hands. "Go eat out. Talk and get a good night's rest. We'll be home bright and early, and then we can talk about my bucket list."

"But I—"

Dad leaned down to whisper in her ear, "She's holding it together for you two, but she needs to rest. We'll be home tomorrow, okay?"

When she nodded, he kissed her temple.

"I'm glad you're home, kiddo."

Violet kissed Lynne's cheek and retreated to the door as Jesse said his goodbyes as well. Once she was in the hallway, she leaned against the wall and closed her eyes. A mixture of dread, sorrow, and worry sloshed around inside of her.

"Are you good?"

She opened her eyes as Jesse reached for her. She straightened and slapped his hand away. "No."

He wasn't allowed to be a monster one moment and her brother the next. She stalked away with her arms wrapped around herself.

The sun began its descent as they walked through the parking lot. Neither of them said a word as they got in the car. Once more, she leaned against the window and prayed she would wake from this nightmare.

"Are you hungry?" Jesse asked.

"No." There was no way she could eat after a day like today.

When he pulled out of the lot, she said, "We should stop at the store."

"For what?"

"Groceries. I doubt they have any."

"I'm beat. We can go tomorrow."

She wanted to argue, but she didn't have the energy. Not a word was said during the mercifully short drive back to the house. As he pulled into the driveway, she said, "You don't have to park. I'm going to run to the store."

"We'll go in the morning," he said as he pulled into the garage.

"I want to do it now." She needed the morning after pill.

"Tomorrow," he said as he shut off the engine and pocketed the keys.

"What the hell, Jesse? I don't need you to come with me," she said as he got out of the car.

"You're dead on your ass. Get in the house."

"Don't tell me—" she began but stopped abruptly when his body language changed. She eyed him through the windshield. Her finger hovered over the lock button, but it would do no good. He had the damn keys.

"Get out of the car, Vi."

Her mind raced as she tried to think of her options, but she didn't have any. She shoved the door open, slammed it, and marched up to him.

"Now what?" she challenged, ready to spit in his face and knee him in the balls if he touched her.

His mouth quirked. "You've changed."

She hadn't changed where it counted. He was more mellow than he'd been when she picked him up from the airport. Was it because they fucked or had seeing Lynne put a damper on his libido? Either way, he wasn't Jesse the psycho, he was Jesse the nice guy, but she didn't trust him. It would only take a second for him to switch into someone else.

"You *haven't* changed," she retorted.

He said nothing. He just stared at her. She couldn't decipher what was going on behind those blue eyes and was too fucking tired to try. When she walked past him, his hand brushed over her hair. She recoiled and raced to her room. She locked the bedroom and bathroom doors and listened. She couldn't hear him coming after her, which meant he stayed in the living area. Hopefully, he would watch TV, leave her the hell alone, and pass out on the couch.

She was thirsty, but not about to go to the kitchen for water. Drinking from the bathroom sink would have to do. Hastily, she washed her face and drank from the faucet before she barricaded the entrances into her room. She wedged her desk chair beneath the doorknob that led to the bathroom and pushed her drawers in front of the other door before she changed into pajama shorts and a college tee. She climbed into bed and collapsed on the plethora of pillows. She took a deep breath and was pleased by the scent of fresh sheets.

She reached for her phone and dialed Reese's number. "Hey."

"Hey." Reese's voice was soft and subdued. "I'm sorry about your mom. Are you okay?"

She blinked rapidly to stop the tears. "No."

"I'm so sorry, Vi. Is there anything I can do?"

She swallowed hard and shook her head before she got out another shaky, "No."

"Me and Meg were talking," Reese said slowly. "We

sprung this move on you out of the blue and now this thing with your mom... Meg and I can stay longer to give you time to figure everything out, so you don't have to worry about moving on top of everything else. We know money's tight, so we'll pay your share of the rent this month. Don't worry about it."

Her heart swelled. "You guys are the best, but you don't have to do that. I'm moving home."

Reese's voice changed. "Home? To Texas?"

"Yes."

"Do you want to? Or do you feel you have to because of your mom?"

"I was thinking about it before I found out she has cancer. Now that I know, I want to be here." She sighed. "I dropped out of college years ago and haven't been able to find my feet. I don't want to go into more debt, and I should be here after..." After Lynne was gone. She still couldn't say it out loud.

"How soon are you going to move?"

She rubbed the space between her brows as she tried to think. "I'll be back within a couple of days. Right now, she's stable, so I want to do this before she declines even more." Her chest ached. "And I know you guys are trying to move out and everything."

"Meg and I can get your stuff sorted."

"That would be wonderful. Thank you."

"Of course."

"I'll keep you posted."

"Please let us know if we can do anything for you."

"Thanks. You guys are the best."

"We love you, Vi."

"Love you too. I'll be in touch."

"Okay. Bye."

She hung up and stared at the ceiling as tears leaked out of the corner of her eyes. When her breath hitched, she flipped onto her stomach and wrapped her arms around a pillow. Her hands fisted as she fought for control, but in the end, she couldn't hold back the tide. She wasn't sure if she was sobbing because of what happened in the SUV and shower or because of the impending death of the only mother she'd ever known.

A part of her registered the smell of cooking sausage, but she ignored it in favor of a much-needed crying spell. When the storm passed and her head felt as if it was going to explode, the doorknob rattled.

"Vi?"

She tensed.

The knob jiggled as Jesse turned it again. "I made dinner."

As if she would eat anything he made for her. "I'm good," she called in a stuffy voice.

"You should eat."

She scowled. Now he was Jesse the nursemaid. He could kiss her ass. "I'm going to sleep."

"I'll save some for you."

Whatever. She exchanged the damp pillow for a dry one and blew her nose as she hugged a blush-colored pillow to her chest and curled into a ball. She'd been so sure she could handle Jesse. She thought she had the balls to stop him from taking advantage and that she would laugh in his face. She wasn't laughing now. He had taken her over so easily.

The way he talked to Dad and Lynne, as if nothing was out of the ordinary, sent a chill down her spine. How did he do that? How could he act as if nothing happened? Why was she curled in a ball in her bedroom while he was eating and probably watching sports on TV? Was there something wrong with her? Why couldn't she shrug off everything like him? Why couldn't she be cool and detached? She hated that he could dissolve her into a blubbering mess. She wasn't a teenager anymore, but she still felt like one. She hadn't changed one damn bit.

---

MASON, HER EX-BOYFRIEND, WAS MAKING LOVE TO HER. He brushed kisses over her face as he did something with his hips that made her arch her back. Whoever he had been with since they broke up had taught him some things. He was showing more technique and finesse than he had when they were together.

Something about that niggled at the back of her mind, but she couldn't focus, not when he was working her just right. Her body hummed as zips of pleasure nipped at her heels. *Yes.* She rarely got off during vaginal sex. She always had to take care of herself later, but Mason was nailing it tonight. He was hitting all the right points while biting her breasts and sucking on her neck. Damn. He upped his game big time. He tilted her hips, going even deeper, and she moaned.

"You forgot the window."

It took a moment for the words to register. Shouldn't he be whispering hot, dirty shit in her ear? What the hell did *'You forgot the window'* mean? Whoever Mason learned these moves from needed to give him lessons in dirty talk.

"You were made for me."

Something wasn't right. Mason's voice wasn't that deep and on second thought, the hands moving over her were rough, calloused. Mason worked at a movie theater. He didn't have the hands of a construction worker.

"That's my good girl."

*Good girl.* Her eyes flew open. It took several seconds for her mind to clear and her vision to adjust to the light. It wasn't Mason fucking her slow and sweet. It was Jesse riding her as if he had every right to. There was a bedside lamp on, and he was as naked as she was.

She braced her hands on his shoulders. "Stop!"

"I told you to spread and even in sleep, you listened to me. You know my voice, my touch. You know *me*, Vi."

"I *don't* know you!"

"Yet your body clutches at mine." He planted himself deep, making her squirm as he pulsed inside her. "God, you're fucking soaked for me. You think locked doors can keep you from me?"

"You're a monster," she whispered.

He switched his rhythm from fucking to hip rolling. His fingers came into play, and she stiffened. Rough, she could handle. Gentleness hurt her in places she couldn't describe. She clawed his back, provoking him so he would go back to the cruel asshole he'd been earlier today. He didn't take the bait. He covered her face with light, teasing kisses that made her lash out. She scored his neck before he pinned her wrist to the mattress.

"Didn't you miss me even a little?" he breathed in her ear.

"No!"

"I missed you. I missed *this*."

His low, earthy groan made her wetter. Fucking hell! He

tucked his face beside hers as he lifted her knees so he could go deeper.

"If I hadn't made a move, we never would have made it here."

She gripped his hair and yanked savagely. "You had no right!"

How many times had her mind replayed a scenario like this? Her pinned to the bed with Jesse over her and her childhood bedroom as the backdrop? But this time he was stronger, she was angrier, and there was no one here to save her.

"I claimed the right," he said against her lips. "And I don't regret it. I still don't."

She bit him, but before she could split his lip, he gripped her jaw, forcing her to release him.

"Bad girl. If you're hungry, I'll give you something to eat."

He slid out of her and crawled up her body. She panicked as his heavy thighs pinned her arms, and he settled on her chest. He stroked himself over her mouth, which was forced open by his hand squeezing her cheeks. She spewed hate from her eyes. He didn't seem bothered. It seemed to arouse him even more. His fist pumped, and she heard him groan a moment before warm cum splattered her mouth and face.

"Fuck yes."

Her limbs jerked as she fought with all her might, but it was no use. He was like a boulder sitting on top of her. She was helpless and at his mercy. He eased his grip on her jaw, allowing her to swallow.

"This brings back memories."

"You're a sick fucker."

He used her pajamas to clean her face. She bared her teeth.

"Will you stop ruining my clothes?"

His teeth gleamed as he stretched out on top of her and tucked his head beneath her chin. "It feels good to be home."

"Get off me!"

His hand moved down her body and slipped inside her. "I almost forgot."

"Don't!"

"If you hadn't pushed me, we both would have got off at the same time," he chided.

"I don't want this!"

"You do."

She fought him, but she fought herself harder. She didn't want to give him this. He didn't deserve it. He was watching her, calculating every flicker of emotion that crossed her face. At first, she tried to play dead. Then, she got physical. She fought with every ounce of strength she had. He rose to the challenge and became hard enough to slip inside her again.

"Why fight this?" he murmured.

"I have to!"

"Why?"

"This is wrong!"

He applied pressure on her G spot, and she moaned.

"Does this feel wrong?"

"Please, please stop," she pleaded.

When he pumped his hips, she let out a choked cry. He fucked her until she was flung into a climax that forced her mouth to open and close like a fish out of water. Her vision flashed white as she came down from the excruciating high.

"That's my girl. Give into me," he praised.

Tears seeped out of her eyes as he continued to fuck her, reviving their dirty past before he came again, planting himself deep and holding himself there. His eyelids were heavy and his breathing ragged as he slumped over her. His hand stroked over her hair as he whispered, "No one compares to you."

# CHAPTER 3

"Get up, Vi."

She opened her eyes. She was on her side, curled into a ball, without a stitch of clothing on. Sunlight streamed through the blinds, revealing Jesse, who stood beside the bed dressed in jeans and a tee. She sat up and reached for the comforter, only to find that it had been tossed on the floor. She hugged a pillow to her chest and glared at him as she brushed her hair out of her eyes. She had a vague recollection of being spoon fucked at some unholy hour this morning.

"Mom and Dad are on their way," he said as he headed to the door.

She stared after him for a minute before her eyes tracked around the room. The dresser had been put back in its place, and the chair she wedged under the doorknob was back at her desk. Her head whipped toward the window. Is that how he came in? Why had the window been unlocked? She shook her head as she tried to clear the cobwebs from her mind. She hobbled to the bathroom and washed herself thoroughly before she stripped the bed and threw her sheets in the wash, desperate to erase any sign of what happened last night.

When she walked into the living room, she found Jesse in the kitchen flipping pancakes. He looked up from the stove.

"Are you hungry?" he asked.

Her hands balled into fists as she stalked toward him. *"Hungry?"*

"You didn't eat last night."

She pounded her fist on the counter. "How do you *do* that?"

"Do what?"

"Act like nothing happened! You..." She jabbed her finger at him, at a loss for words. Her eyes burned with tears, but she refused to let them fall. Her tears and pleas had no effect on him. "You *fucked* me!"

His eyes moved over her. "Yes."

Her mouth dropped open. "Yes? That's all you have to say?"

"What do you want me to say?"

Her hands opened and closed as she tried to articulate what she wanted from him. She had never confronted him or talked about his assaults in the light of day. She had taken her cue from him and never said a word, always acting like nothing was going on, but things were different now. *She* was different. She wanted to fight. "What the fuck is wrong with you?"

"You swear a lot," he said mildly.

She smacked the counter so hard, her hand tingled. "Stop treating me like a kid and answer me!"

"What's the question?"

She was so pissed, she was shaking. She went toe to toe with him. "What kind of person does what you do to me?"

His eyes moved over her face. "I told you yesterday."

"Told me what?"

His finger trailed down her throat. "I can't stop."

She stepped back and clutched her neck to banish the effect his touch had on her. "You have to."

He said nothing, he just watched her.

"Is... is this your thing?"

"Thing?" he echoed as he slid a hot pancake onto a growing stack.

She was miffed to see they were all perfectly round and golden.

"You force women? That's your thing?"

He visibly stiffened. "I don't force women."

"You force *me*, jackass."

He turned from her. "You're different."

Butter sizzled as he whipped pancake batter and poured it in the pan. Her stomach rumbled, but she wasn't going to be distracted by food.

"How am I different?" she challenged.

He didn't answer.

"I think you have multiple personality disorder," she announced.

"You think so?"

His lack of reaction enraged her.

"Yes! There's something wrong with you, Jesse! You need help! I also think you have a taboo fetish."

He paused in the middle of buttering pancakes. "Fetish?"

"Yes. That's why you're fixated on me." She waved her hand as she tried to find the right words. "You get off on our relation to one another. It has nothing to do with me. If I wasn't your stepsister, I'd be nothing to you."

His eyes narrowed, but the words were finally coming, so she didn't stop. She had to get this out.

"You like the risk of being caught. That's why you did it in the car yesterday and why in the light of day." She gestured to the sunlight streaming through the windows. "You can act perfectly normal. You—"

It happened so fast; she didn't have time to run. One second, he was standing beside the stove and the next, he was on her. He gripped her face before he kissed her. She screamed and beat her fists against his chest as he backed her against the fridge. The cool metal was a shocking contrast to her feverish skin.

"I fucked you in the SUV because I couldn't wait another second to have you again." His hand fisted in her hair and pulled, bearing her throat to him. "And I can act normal right now because I've had you enough times that I can think straight. But, if you want more, I'm ready."

When he arched against her, she went rigid. He was rock hard. How was that possible?

"We could go to a foreign country where no one knows us and get a hotel room for a month. I'd fuck you so many times, you'd forget your name." He bit her jaw and then licked away the sting. "It has nothing to do with a fetish and everything to do with you. The compulsion I have to get you on your back doesn't care that our parents are down the hall or that someone could discover us in a parking lot, a field, or at church."

When his hand went to her jeans, she gripped his wrist.

"Don't."

"I don't want you because you're my stepsister. I want you because you're you. I wanted you from the start, but you refused to see."

He undid the button and shoved his hand into her jeans, despite her attempts to stop him.

"So, I forced you," he said against her ear as his fingers slipped inside her. Tension eased from him, as if he had stuck his cock in her. He sighed and rubbed his face in her hair. "I should feel bad, but I don't. You make me feel too damn good to regret what I've done."

She shuddered as he worked her roughly. "Jesse."

"You like that? You like what I do to you?"

"Stop!"

He glared at her, face carved with lust, anger, and determination.

"Five years, Vi. Five years you stayed away. You want to diagnose me? Paint me as a monster? I can take it. I'll take anything as long as I get this."

As he rubbed her clit, she hissed through her teeth. He groaned and withdrew his fingers. In seconds, he had his pants undone and was sliding into her wet heat.

"Years, I've dreamed of this. No one came close."

His tongue stroked hers and when she tried to turn her face away, he braced a hand against her cheek.

"How can you deny what's between us?" he asked hoarsely.

The fridge began to move as he hammered into her, so he transferred his grip to the metal box to hold it steady. The sound of the garage door opening made her stiffen.

"Jesse! They're back!"

His eyes gleamed with maniacal recklessness. "You want to tell them, Vi?"

"No!" She shoved at him, but he wouldn't budge. "We have to stop!"

"Make me."

She stared at him, absolutely horrified.

"You could have stopped me anytime. All you had to do was tell them what I was doing to you. Why didn't you?"

"I... You—" She heard the garage door close and wailed, "Jesse!"

"Your choice, Violet."

She squirmed in panic before she yanked his mouth to hers and kissed him. He stiffened, shocked for a moment, before he moaned. She sucked on his tongue as she gripped his ass and pulled him closer. She milked him desperately. He punched the fridge as he came.

"Fuck!"

The moment he was finished, she shoved him. When he staggered back, she pulled up her pants and slipped past him. She started toward the garage, but turned when she didn't hear him move. He had both hands braced on the fridge and his pants were around his ankles.

"Jesse!"

She dashed back to him and pulled up his pants and zipped and buttoned them.

"You're such a fucker," she spat as she turned off the stove and ran to the garage just as the door opened.

"Morning!" Lynne called as she entered, leaning heavily on her father.

"Hi," Violet said hoarsely as she smoothed a hand over her hair and then her neck, which was damp from Jesse's saliva. "How are you feeling?"

"Better with you two here," Lynne chirped.

"Mom." Jesse brushed against Violet as he leaned over to kiss Lynne's cheek. "Hungry?"

"Bags in the car?" Violet asked Dad, who nodded.

She escaped to the garage. When the door swung shut, she slumped against the wall. She was shaking. How the hell did that confrontation backfire so badly?

"Jesse, you made pancakes. My favorite!" Lynne crowed.

Violet shook her head as she retrieved the bags from the trunk.

---

BREAKFAST PASSED WITHOUT A HITCH UNTIL THE WASHER BEEPED to announce her load was done.

"Someone's washing clothes?" Lynne asked.

"I tossed in my sheets," Violet said as casually as possible.

Lynne frowned. "You're washing your sheets? I changed them right before you came."

She willed herself to stay calm as she said, "I spilled soda in bed last night." She refused to look at Jesse, even though she sensed his amusement. Fucking asshole.

"Oh no! I hoped they didn't stain. You always loved that comforter."

She made a noncommittal noise. On second thought, she should have stained those damn sheets long ago so she could get new ones. Once she moved home, she would repaint the walls and change out everything, so there were no reminders of Jesse and the past.

Despite Lynne gushing about how tasty breakfast was, she ate only five bites before she needed to lay down. Violet helped Dad get Lynne settled and hung her bedsheets on the clothesline to dry while she tossed her parent's things in the wash and started a new load. She cleaned up the kitchen and saw Jesse standing on the driveway, greeting friends who stopped by to welcome him home. Nothing had changed.

*You could have stopped me anytime. All you had to do was tell them what I was doing to you. Why didn't you?*

He knew damn well why she hadn't told anyone. Why did he make it sound as if she encouraged his advances, as if she *wanted* him? She tossed the dishes in the sink with more force than was necessary and was instantly contrite when Dad appeared in the hallway with a frown.

"Sorry," she mouthed.

Dad shook his head before he disappeared back into the bedroom. Violet washed the dishes, put away the food, and grabbed the car keys. She tiptoed to her parent's door. Dad was reading in bed with Mom's head on his lap. The scene tugged at her heartstrings. He peered at her over his glasses.

"I'm going out," Violet whispered.

"Where?" he asked in a low voice.

"I'm going to run to the store. Do you need anything?"

"No. Do you need money?"

She did, but she wasn't going to take any from him. "No, I'm good. I'll see you in a bit."

As she walked out of the hallway, Jesse came through the front door with a friend.

"Violet!"

She smiled as Blaine wrapped her in a hug. She caught a glimpse of Jesse's narrowed eyes before she pulled away.

"I see you even less than Jesse," Blaine said as he stepped back to take her in. "How've you been?"

"Good. And you?"

He puffed out his chest. "Four kids."

She blinked. "How is that possible?"

Jesse snickered as Blaine said, "Two sets of twins."

"Oh my God!"

Blaine shrugged. "They're a blast. You should come over. Allison hasn't seen you since high school."

"Maybe I will," she said, even though she wouldn't. "It's good to see you."

"Likewise."

Violet used her thumb to point to the garage. "I'm heading out. We'll catch up later?"

"Sure."

As she made her escape, she saw Jesse point Blaine toward the living room before he started after her. She tried to slam the door in his face, but he stuck his combat boot in the opening and shoved his way in.

"What?" Violet snapped when he loomed over her.

"Where are you going?"

"To the store. Is that against the law?"

"For what?"

She bared her teeth at him. "None of your business."

He grasped her chin. "You should know by now, everything you do is my business."

She slapped his hand away. "I can take care of myself."

"Don't do anything stupid," he warned before he brushed a kiss over her parted lips and headed back in the house.

She didn't move for a full minute. He never touched or kissed her unless he intended to fuck her, so what was that? She let out an aggravated growl and slammed the car door when she got in. She couldn't take a full breath until she put a few miles between herself and the house.

What game was he playing? What happened in the kitchen filled her with cold terror. He couldn't want to be discovered. It would destroy their family. Their parents were devout Christians who didn't believe in premarital sex, much less a sexual relationship between two kids they had raised as siblings. It was blasphemous and yet in less than 24 hours of being home, they were closer to being discovered than they had ever been in high school. What the fuck was he thinking? He would ruin their lives, and their family would never be the same. Why court such stupid risks?

She walked into Planned Parenthood, accepted a clipboard with a questionnaire, and took a seat. Was she sexually active? *Yes.* (But not by choice.) Was there a chance she could have an STD? *Yes.* (Who knew what the hell he did on base?). What was she here for? *Test for STDs, morning after pill, and birth control.*

The waiting room wasn't full, which was a good sign. She pulled out her phone and went through the group text with Meg and Reese, who took pictures of her belongings and asked if she wanted to keep, sell, or toss. She met Reese and Meg in Algebra in her freshmen year of college. They moved out of the dorms and rented a house, where they'd been for four years. Reese and Meg had recently graduated and were both happy in their careers.

Out of their trio, she was the screw-up. Her friends encouraged her to go back to school, recommended better jobs, and urged her toward good, upstanding men, but nothing good lasted long. Meg and Reese tried their best, but they couldn't make her better. She had short spurts of motivation that put her on the straight and narrow, but it was only a matter of time before she reverted to bad habits that kept her from advancing in life. It was no wonder they were moving out. She was holding them back. Reese was engaged, and Meg had been with the same guy for two years. They were going to marry, have kids, and excel in their careers while she moved home and watched her mother die.

"Violet Carr?"

She pocketed her phone and approached the nurse,

who waved her to the back with an impatient look. The nurse repeated questions she had already answered on her paperwork before she was weighed and directed to a room where she was ordered to strip and wait for a doctor.

While she waited, she continued to answer Reese and Meg about what to do with her things. God, by the time she got back, they would have it all sorted. She checked the flights and winced when she saw the price. There weren't affordable flights to Salt Lake City this week. She checked her credit card statement to see what wiggle room she had. The ticket would max out one of her credit cards, leaving an alarmingly small margin on the others. She needed a job ASAP.

An unfamiliar number popped up on the screen. She ignored it and frowned when the number reappeared a minute later. It wasn't a Utah or Texas number, so she rejected it again. She shivered and clamped her thighs together beneath the thin paper sheet draped over her lap. Why did they make these rooms so cold?

When Dad's number appeared on the screen, she eyed the closed door before she answered.

"Hey, Dad."

"Where are you?"

She jerked. "Jesse?"

"I called you twice."

How the hell was she supposed to know his number? And why the hell would she answer his call? "What do you want?"

"You've been gone over an hour. Where are you?"

"Does Dad need me?"

"Where are you?"

The door opened, and a doctor came in with a clipboard and a smile. "Violet Carr?"

She hung up. "Yes. Hi."

"How are you feeling?" the doctor asked.

"Good," she said, and switched the phone to silent when it began to ring. "Sorry."

She tossed the phone in her purse and tried to shrug off her irritation. Here she was, trying to take care of business, and he was trying to track her down. Why did he care where she was? Did he think she was going to jump off a bridge? She smothered her temper and focused on the doctor, who wanted more details about her sex life.

As she approached the house, she saw a crowd gathered on the driveway. Mr. Popular was holding court. Everyone moved aside so she could park in the garage. She waved as she passed, taking in the familiar faces. Her heart sank as she turned off the car. She knew they would expect her to chat with them, but she had never felt less like socializing. Nevertheless, appearances needed to be kept up.

She mentally braced as she walked out of the garage. She was immediately engulfed in a round of hugs and kisses. She and Jesse being only one year apart meant they knew each other's friends, even though they ran with different crowds. Jesse played every sport he could, while she was pulled into student government by her friends and ended up becoming heavily involved in the school newspaper. She wasn't an introvert or an extrovert, but somewhere in between. She didn't seek the spotlight and preferred to stay behind the scenes organizing. All of that changed in her junior year. When Jesse ruined their relationship, she withdrew from everyone. He effectively isolated her in a world of her own where she had no one, and she would never forgive him for it.

"God, Vi, you're looking *good*," Brody drawled.

She looked him up and down. "You're not looking so bad yourself."

He tossed an arm over her shoulder and drew her against his side. "Dinner?"

Jesse stood across from them. She couldn't read his expression since he wore dark sunglasses, but she got the distinct impression that he didn't like what was happening. Good. Anything that pissed him off made her happy. He had always been an overprotective older brother, even before their sexual relationship began. In her junior year, he went ballistic when he caught her with her boyfriend, Tucker. That was the day everything changed.

She gave Brody an apologetic smile. "Can I take a rain check? I need to spend time with my mom."

"Right." Brody sobered and jerked his head at the house. "My mom heard you two were back. She sent me over here with a casserole."

"Aw, that's so sweet."

"How long are you here for?"

She focused on Marissa, the girl at Jesse's side. Marissa was his middle school girlfriend who had never gotten over him.

"I'm not sure," she said.

"Jesse says you're moving back," Marissa persisted.

Violet eyed Jesse, who had the military stance down pat. "Yes, I am."

"You looking for a job? My mom's shop needs a sales associate."

"I might take you up on that."

Hours passed as they stood on the driveway, catching up on life. She had dodged these people, convinced they would be able to sense what was happening if she spent too much time with them. She was surprised to hear herself laugh and banter with them. They treated her like one of the pack, even though she had cut herself off from them long ago. They brought up happy memories that had been overshadowed by the filth Jesse wrought in her life. Her hopes and dreams died when Jesse painted her world in shades of gray. He made her an outcast. She struggled to make true connections with people because she couldn't let anyone know her secret.

As Marissa caught her up on all their friends' marriages, she constructed a mental flowchart that would come in handy since she was moving back. The easy camaraderie between all of them banished her anxieties and made her feel almost normal. People came and went, and she made plans to get together with all of them and by God, she was going to keep her promise. Jesse may have fucked up her teenage years, but she couldn't let him ruin her future as well. She was going to start over. She had people rooting for her, people who wanted to help and reconnect with her. None of them thought it was embarrassing that she was moving home. They were excited to have her back. By the time the last person left, the sun had set, and she and Jesse were left standing beneath the orange streetlights.

"Where did you go today?" he asked.

She walked away from him.

"Vi."

She rounded the SUV and heard the garage door coming down. As she reached the steps that led into the house, Jesse spun her around to face him.

"*What?*"

"Where did you go?" he demanded.

"I told you I was going to the store."

He glanced in the car. "Where's your bags?"

"What do you care?"

"Where," he enunciated slowly and deliberately as he hauled her close, "did you go?"

She lifted her chin. "Planned Parenthood."

He stiffened. "For what?"

"Are you serious?" She wrenched away from him. "I got an STD test and the morning after pill, jackass."

"STD test?"

"I don't know what the hell you do at your base!"

He scowled. "I'm not fucking anyone else."

"Fuck you," she snapped as she marched into the house and tried to slam the door in his face.

She poked her head in her parent's bedroom and heard the shower going. She decided to do the same and locked both doors before she stripped and stepped under the spray. She had been in Texas for two days, but it felt like two weeks. Her mind bounced from one thing to the next. She had so much to do. She had to wrap up her life in Utah, spend as much time as possible with Lynne, steer clear of Jesse's bullying ass, and get a job. By going to Utah, she could accomplish two of her goals—tie up a loose end and dodge Jesse. Avoiding him was paramount in her mind.

After she dressed, she went to her parent's room again to find Jesse sitting beside Mom. They were talking in low tones and Lynne's face was drawn with worry. She left to give them privacy and found that someone had brought her sheets in from the line and hung the second load. She made her bed before going into the dining room to find Dad eating at the table.

"Okay?" she asked.

"Yeah." He ran a hand down his face. "Nice to see your friends come by."

"They're Jesse's friends."

"And yours."

She couldn't refute that, not after what she experienced today. She braced her arms on the back of a chair. "Marissa says she can hook me up with a job at her mom's shop."

Dad frowned. "You don't need to work."

"I do," she mumbled.

"Violet."

She held up both hands. "I told you, I got myself in trouble."

"How much do you need?"

"No, Dad."

"Tell me."

"I don't want you paying my bills."

"I don't want you working right now. Lynne needs us here."

She grimaced.

"Tell me how much."

She waved a hand. "I don't need it right now."

"Then let me know when you have a figure."

She took the seat beside him and grabbed a fork to dig into the dish in front of him. "Brody's mom's casserole?"

"Yep."

"She's an angel."

"Brody's a good guy."

She paused in mid munch and raised her brows. "What?"

"Brody." Dad looked a tad uncomfortable as he speared a broccoli. "He has a good job and took care of his mom and siblings after his dad died."

"Dad," she said repressively.

"Just saying."

She shook her head. "Wow."

When Jesse appeared and took the chair on Dad's other side, she left the table. She headed down the hallway and was relieved to see Lynne sitting up in bed.

"Mom?"

Lynne gave her a welcoming smile. "Hi, honey."

Violet sat beside her and examined her closely. "How are you feeling?"

Lynne ignored her questions and patted her knee. "Dad tells me you're moving home?"

"Yes."

"It's not working out in Utah?" Lynne asked sympathetically.

She shook her head.

"I can't deny I'm relieved you're coming home. Dad's going to need company after I'm gone."

She flinched. "Please don't talk like that. I haven't even begun to process all of this yet."

"You'll be fine."

Her eyes burned with tears. "How can you say that?"

Lynne cupped her chin. "Because I know you. You're a sensible girl with a good heart. You know when to throw in the towel and come home. You're the rock your father needs."

She wanted to believe in Lynne's view of her, but knew it was false. How could she be a rock for her father when she couldn't stand up for herself? And the good heart Lynne believed she possessed had been corrupted by Jesse long ago.

"Do you have a lot to do in Utah?"

She nodded. "I think I should go back and get it all sorted. Is that okay?"

"Of course. It'll give us all peace of mind and when you come back, we can go to Florida!"

"Florida?"

"Yes, remember that trip? It was the best! I think about it all the time. I want to swim in the ocean and get some sun. That's second on my bucket list, right behind you and Jesse being home. What do you think?"

"Going to Florida sounds wonderful."

Lynne beamed. "As soon as you get back, we'll plan. The faster you wrap up everything in Utah, the sooner we can go."

"Great."

"How long do you think you'll be?"

"I'm not sure, but my friends are already helping me get my things together."

Lynne's brows drew together. "How are you getting your car here? Or are you going to sell it?"

"I'll pack it up and drive it here."

"That's too far, Violet."

"It'll just take a day or two," she said with a shrug.

She was looking forward to the long drive. She needed some alone time to get her head straight and come to terms with everything.

"Jesse should go with you," Lynne said.

She jolted. "No! I got this."

"Violet," Lynne said, sounding much more like the mother she remembered. "I don't want you doing this all by yourself."

"I'm twenty-three!"

"So?"

As she scrambled to come up with more excuses, she heard, "When do you want to leave?"

She turned to see Jesse leaning against the doorjamb. He looked as if he had been there for some time.

"I'm fine," she said in a flat tone that told him to butt out.

"Did you book your flight already?" he asked.

"No, I—"

"I'll do it."

When he disappeared down the hallway, she shot up from the bed. "Hey!"

Lynne chuckled. "You two," she said fondly. "Always bickering."

She would have taken exception to that, but there were more urgent matters to see to. She charged into Jesse's room and found him sitting on the edge of the bed with his phone in hand. He looked up as she came in.

"Do you want to leave first thing in the morning?" he asked.

She was lightheaded with rage. "You're not coming with me."

"Mom doesn't want you driving all that way by your-self. Dad won't let you, either."

"I'm grown!"

"I want to sleep in a bit. How about a ten o'clock flight?"

"You aren't coming with me," she said through clenched teeth.

"I think we should leave mid-morning," he said absently as he scrolled.

"Jesse!"

He looked up. "We don't have much time. Mom wants to go to Florida, and the only thing stopping her is you. We'll get your shit and drive back. We'll be gone three days max."

"You don't know what I need to do there!" He was taking over and ruining her plans, as usual.

"We'll handle it when we get there."

She snatched his phone and hid it behind her back. "There's no *we*. I'm doing this by myself."

He rose. "You aren't. Give me my phone."

She felt a modicum of safety since their parents were present. She took a step toward the door as she said, "Mom needs you here."

"Mom needs us both here. She isn't going to be able to relax if she's worrying about you. The sooner we leave, the sooner we can come back and enjoy ourselves."

"Enjoy?" she choked.

His eyes narrowed. "You're stalling."

Hell yes, she was stalling. She was trying to get away from him, not have him invade more of her life than he already had. "You aren't—"

He shoved her against the wall and pinned her there with his body.

"Back up," she hissed.

"I'm going with you," he said, voice equally low. "You can throw a tantrum, but Mom and Dad will back me up. You're not doing that long drive by yourself."

"You're trying to take over!"

His eyes moved over her face and then focused on her lips. "You can give in, or we can fight. Either way, I'll win."

Motherfucker. No matter how she resisted, he always triumphed. Circumstances hemmed her in, but he couldn't win every battle. Eventually, he had to leave, and she would move on with her life. She held his gaze as she tossed his phone. He didn't move a muscle as they listened to it tumble across the carpet. She lost this fight, but she didn't intend to lose more if she could help it.

"If you insist," she drawled.

"I do," he said, eyes still on her mouth.

"Suit yourself." If he wanted to book the tickets, he could pay for them, and she could give her credit card a breather.

"Mid-morning?" he asked, voice low and gravelly.

"Yes. Now, back off."

For a moment, he didn't move. She could hear the TV in the living room and the faint sound of Lynne's snores. She couldn't read Jesse's expression, but she felt his erection between them. She silently dared him to make a move. She would castrate him if he touched her with their parent's present.

He reached out and fingered her hair. "Your STD test will come back negative. I wouldn't put you at risk like that."

Before she could digest that, he turned from her to retrieve his phone.

"I'll book the tickets."

She slipped out of his room, went into her own, and locked the door. She leaned against it, put her hands over her face, and stifled a scream.

# CHAPTER 4



"THIS MUST BE A NICE BREAK FROM THE COLD," DAD SAID. "Two years in Alaska? I don't know if I could do that."

"It wasn't too bad," Jesse said. "But I'm glad to be home."

They were on their way to the airport and despite the early hour, Dad and Jesse were way too fucking chipper. She woke with a headache that was getting worse by the second.

"I'm glad you're here to help Violet with her move," Dad continued. "I would have gone with her if I could."

"No problem. I don't mind," Jesse said easily.

She glared at the back of his seat. Jesse was always winning brownie points, while she came off looking ungrateful and churlish. Mom and Dad were clearly relieved that Jesse was accompanying her on this trip. She'd been hoping to regroup in Utah, and now her plan was in ruins. She spent most of the night examining her situation from all sides, trying to find a way out, but there was none. She half-expected Jesse to sneak into her room. Their parent's presence hadn't stopped him in the past, but wonder of wonders, he hadn't intruded. Couldn't he give her a heads-up so she could get a decent night of sleep? She tried to doze, but the sound of Jesse's voice kept her alert.

When Dad pulled up to the curb, she stepped out and slammed the door with more force than was necessary, not that anyone noticed. Dad gave her a one-armed hug.

"Wrap it up and hurry home." She gave his waist a squeeze and was about to step away when he added, "And don't give Jesse any hassles."

Her head snapped up. She opened her mouth to argue, but Dad had already turned to Jesse and clapped him on the back.

"Thanks for doing this. Keep an eye on her," Dad said.

"Of course."

She stalked away from them and headed to the check-in kiosk. She tapped the screen before she realized she didn't have the itinerary details. As she stood there, a big hand reached past her and began to type. She gritted her teeth and stepped aside as Jesse claimed their tickets and surrendered her duffel and his backpack. When he headed toward TSA, she trailed behind, hoping he would get impatient and go on without her. He didn't. He waited patiently and stayed by her side. As soon as she got through security, she made a beeline for the nearest coffee shop. When she finished ordering, Jesse added his drink and two breakfast sandwiches as well. She glared at him until he handed over his credit card. She didn't thank him as she went to the end of the counter to wait for the coffee that would make her feel better.

As she stared intently at the barista's, Jesse shuffled her to the side so some man could grab his coffee.

"He was behind us," she grouched.

"He ordered black coffee," Jesse explained.

She glanced up to find him smiling at her. She scowled. "What's so funny?"

"You are." He brushed her hair back. "You're still not a morning person."

As she shied away from his touch, she bumped into a table. As she apologized to the startled couple, Jesse swept her under his arm and drew her against him.

"You need someone to keep you out of trouble."

She elbowed his hard abs. "*You're* trouble. I've been fine on my own!"

"That's debatable, baby."

"Don't call me—"

"Iced caramel coffee for Violet!" the barista called.

She broke off to fetch her drink. She stabbed her straw in and took a sip. Everything else faded away. She was about to skip out of the shop when Jesse grabbed her arm.

"We stay together," he said.

"I'm not a kid," she mumbled around her straw.

"Sometimes you act like one."

"Speak for yourself," she retorted, but it wasn't said with enough heat since she was distracted by her drink. She closed her eyes as coffee raced through her veins and awakened her senses. She was deaf and dumb until she got her morning joe.

Once Jesse collected his drink and food, he led the way to their gate. They had less than thirty minutes until boarding time. She chose a seat five down from him and gave him a disgruntled look when he got up and took the seat beside her. Seriously. He was beyond annoying. She did what she did best and ignored him as she savored her coffee and people watched.

There were quite a few interesting characters to examine. A woman in head-to-toe designer labels strutted past.

Even though it was summer, she wore a coat, scarves, and a hat. She must be heading to Antarctica. A few people wearing pajamas and looking as tired as she felt ambled by. A group of hippies wearing androgynous clothing floated past with contented smiles.

Austin hosted an eclectic mix of people who were committed to the city slogan: *Keep Austin Weird*. Austin was the Music Capital of the World and home to many creatives and techies. The vibe in Austin was laidback and open with an undercurrent of Southern hospitality, tradition, and old school values.

A group of girls passed, laughing loudly enough to capture Violet's attention. Their eyes were on Jesse. She glanced at him and inwardly snorted. He was too busy eating to notice the teenagers eyeing him as if he were on a menu. His strong, classic features had always attracted females. Yeah, he was good-looking, but his heart was fucking black. If people only knew... Her mind conjured up an image of Marissa doing everything in her power to get his attention yesterday. Jesse dated his fair share of girls during school, but he hadn't dated anyone his senior year.

She didn't want to talk to him, but curiosity got the better of her. "Does Marissa come around every time you come home?"

When he turned to her, she realized he was too damn close. She scooted as far as her chair would allow, which wasn't more than an inch. Stupid, small, uncomfortable airport seats.

"Marissa and I are friends. You know that," he said.

"She doesn't see you that way."

He gave her an odd look. "Are you jealous?"

She blinked. "Jealous?"

"Why are you asking about her?"

"I think you two would make a great couple." She paused and then added, "And if you got some, you'd leave me the hell alone."

When he leaned toward her, she tensed.

"No one holds any appeal in comparison to you."

"You're sick."

He moved even closer. Her hand itched to slap him.

"You're sick with me," he said as his eyes tracked over her face. "You can't deny it, not when I make you come so hard, you can't even scream."

Her pussy spasmed even as her heart withered in shame. Arousal and anger warred inside her. His mouth curved as if he knew the response he elicited from her body. She considered splashing his cocky face with coffee, but she wasn't sure it was worth the sacrifice. In the end, she looked away from him.

"I hate you."

"You don't," he said as he took the lid off his steaming cup of coffee. "You want to, but you can't."

"Don't tell me I don't when I do," she hissed.

"Want me to prove you wrong?"

"Touch me and I'll kill you." The aroma of his black coffee made her grimace. "How can you drink hot coffee when it's so warm?" It could be snowing, and she'd still order iced coffee.

"When you're in Alaska, you learn to treasure heat in any form. I'm going to drink hot coffee for the rest of my life. I can still feel the cold."

"Too bad you weren't eaten by a polar bear," she mumbled.

"If I was eaten by a polar bear, who would eat you?"

She squeezed her plastic cup, which caused her lid to pop off. "Shut up!"

His eyes laughed at her over the rim of his cup. "So touchy," he taunted.

She leaned in close and was pleased when he tensed. She wanted to wipe that fucking smirk off his face. She made her eyes heavy-lidded as she purred, "I've met a lot of men who know what they're doing in the bedroom. Don't give yourself so much credit."

She put her hand on the arm of the chair in preparation to stand, but the hand that clamped on her thigh stopped her.

"You're brave in public, baby," he said in a flat tone that warned her he was at the end of his rope.

She didn't give a damn how close he was to losing it. Hundreds of people were around. He couldn't do shit to her. "Get your hand off me."

His fingers flexed. "That reminds me. I heard what Dad said about Brody." His eyes bored into hers. "Don't."

The silky warning made her tense. "Don't what?"

"You know," he said mildly as he set his cup on the ground, scanned the crowd, and then looked back at her. "Don't test me."

"You're a fucking psycho!"

He shrugged. "Maybe."

"There's no maybe about it. You can't tell me what to do. I'll date Brody if I want to!"

She wasn't prepared for him to grip her hair. As she opened her mouth to protest, his lips collided with hers. His other hand spread across her cheek, concealing from passersby that she was resisting. He went deep, shoving foreign flavors in her mouth, effectively canceling the taste of caramel that lingered on her tongue.

"I can give you what you need," he said against her mouth and bit her lower lip. "No one comes between us."

Her hand hit his chest, nails digging in when he refused to let her go. "There is no *us.*"

"There's always been an us, you're just too fucking stubborn to see."

"Let me go."

"For now," he whispered and brushed a kiss over her cheek before he released her.

Immediately, she leapt to her feet. As she strode away, she heard, "Coward."

That stopped her in her tracks, but she didn't turn around. She stalked to the bathroom with her hands clenched into fists. She slammed herself into a stall, sat, and buried her face in her hands. How the fuck was he always getting the better of her? She was supposed to be cutting him down to size, making him squirm, and feel remorse for everything he'd done. Instead, he was still pulling the strings and needling the fuck out of her. How was that possible? She was rattled, there was no denying it. She had shut down tons of assholes. What made him different from the others?

To start, no one dared what he did. Jesse was unpredictable and had a huge, unfair advantage. He had known her since she was thirteen and used everything he had learned over the years against her. Motherfucker. Everything was happening too fast for her to plan an attack. He was doing what he did best—keeping her unbalanced and playing defense. Bastard.

She wasn't sure how long she stayed in the bathroom, but by the time she emerged, most of the seats in their section had been emptied as everyone boarded the plane. She didn't look at Jesse as she grabbed her bag. She texted Abel, Reese's fiancé, who would be picking them up at the airport and got an immediate reply as she waited in line.

She was very aware of Jesse standing beside her, cool as a cucumber. She wanted to rake her nails down his face.

The wait to get on the plane seemed to take forever. When she reached her row, she was miffed to see it wasn't a three-seater. She'd been hoping to negotiate with a stranger to sit between them. No luck. She needed a damn break from Jesse, but once again, there was no escape. She collapsed in the window seat while he took the seat beside her. She was on a plane for the second time in three days with her stepbrother beside her. Never in her wildest dreams had she pictured this scenario.

Change entered her life with the force of a freight train. She was in the boxing ring trying to duck the worst of the blows, but she was bruised and bloody and struggling to stay on her feet. How much time did Lynne have? What would happen to her father after Lynne passed? He retired a few years ago and had spent most of his time fixing up the house, biding his time until Lynne retired from teaching second grade. They had pins on the map of future road trips they planned and now... Now, everything had changed in such a way that she still had trouble accepting it.

Lynne was the only mother she'd ever known. She had a vague recollection of her biological mother who left in the middle of the night when she was two. No note, no warning. Just, here today, gone the next. Dad never said a word about her leaving. She took her cue from him and acted as if she had never existed. Since her father was a firefighter, he relied heavily on the church community to look after her when he was working. She hopped from home to home until Lynne came into their lives.

Before Lynne, she had no idea how to be a girl. Dad raised her the best he could, but he was clueless where females were concerned. He had no advice for her. She'd been a wild tomboy and not popular by any means. Lynne taught her how to dress and showered her with love and affection, which she couldn't get enough of. Jesse mirrored his mother. It was natural for him to put his arm around her or cuddle with her on the couch while watching a movie. He used to play with her hair so much that Lynne taught him how to braid it, which he used to do before school.

She glanced at Jesse, who was watching a man trying to stuff the already full overhead bin with one more bag. His features were so heartbreakingly familiar. He was her best friend before he became her enemy. It hurt to look at him.

The first three years with Jesse and Lynne were magical. The four of them fit together as if they had always been. They went on trips and since she and Jesse were only a year apart, she had someone to look out for her in school. Everything seemed idyllic. Lynne was the best stepmom she could ask for, and Jesse was the best big brother... until he wasn't.

He turned his head and speared her with those sky-blue eyes that made her feel as if she were being dissected. She sat back and closed her eyes as the flight attendants launched into their safety demonstration and the plane began to move.

Her eyes burned with tears as the past played behind her closed eyelids. They used to spend every waking hour together. His charisma guaranteed that he was popular in school. He brought her under his wing and made her feel like she belonged for the first time in her life. They did everything together—school, camping, church, family trips, and everything in between. His friends were her friends and vice versa. He was her everything, and before he flipped the script on her, she thought he loved her just as much as she did him. How wrong she'd been.

He was her boogie man, the monster under the bed, and yet here he was in broad daylight. He had been so cruel and heartless, ignoring her wants for his own gratification. He turned her bright future into ash and cast dark shadows over everything she did. She had no drive or ambition, couldn't hold down a job, and had a hard time connecting with people. She didn't do commitment and found it hard to trust anyone. How could she after what she experienced with Jesse? She hadn't been able to shrug off the past and move on as he had.

Her knee bounced as she tried to control her emotions. When a large hand landed on her thigh, she froze. Her eyes popped open. She swiped at her brimming eyes and smacked his offending hand.

"Don't touch me."

"What's wrong?"

"What's right?" she sassed back.

"You're worried about your move?"

She clenched her teeth as the plane left the ground, making her tummy flip. "That's the least of my problems." She brushed away an errant tear. "How long have you known Mom has cancer?"

"Six months."

She jolted. "Six months? Why didn't you tell me?"

He held her furious gaze. "You wouldn't have answered my call."

"That's not the point."

"What is the point?"

Her hands balled into fists. "I should have been told."

"Why?"

"So, I would have time to wrap my mind around all this.

So, I would know everything's going to change and spend more time with her..." Her voice broke off as emotion got the better of her. She swallowed hard and looked out the window so he wouldn't see her face. "I should have been told at the same time as you."

When he took her hand and twined their fingers together, she tried to jerk away, but his hold was solid. "What the hell are you doing?"

"Relax."

"I am relaxed!" she snapped.

He gave her a steady look that made her feel as if she were being childish. He was acting like the supportive older brother she needed but couldn't trust. He was switching personalities again, jockeying for the position that would aid his cause, which was what? She wanted him to be consistently vile or nice. She couldn't handle him playing both sides.

"I don't want you touching me."

He sat back and closed his eyes. She dug her nails into the back of his hand, but he didn't move.

"Jesse."

He appeared to be asleep. She gave her hand another experimental tug, but only got their hands moved from his lap to hers. She stared at their interlocked fingers and felt something inside of her tear.

Past and present clashed, leaving her emotionally shattered. She didn't have time to fortify her walls or regain her composure. She was stripped and stranded in the middle of a storm. All she could do was buckle down and hope she didn't break before it was over.

---

By the time they arrived in Salt Lake City, she felt worse than ever. She hadn't been able to get a wink of sleep, not when her mind was racing a million miles a minute. Thankfully, Jesse slept the whole way and only woke once they touched down.

She led the way to the baggage claim and bought another coffee as soon as she could. She didn't argue when Jesse shouldered his pack and her duffel. She pulled out her phone to text Abel as they exited through the double doors into the sunshine.

It was warm, but Utah didn't have the blanket of humidity that Texas did. She stood at the curb and searched the lineup of cars for Abel's as she sipped her second iced coffee of the day.

"Why Salt Lake City?"

She ignored his question until he tugged on her hair. "What's your problem?"

"Why Salt Lake?" he asked again.

"Why not Salt Lake?"

"What's here that isn't in Texas?"

She held his gaze as she said, "It's about what *isn't* here."

His eyes narrowed. "Meaning?"

"I wanted away from you, away from anyone who knows you." She tipped her face up to the sun. "The fact that I fell in love with the city was a bonus."

"Did running away work?"

Temper canceled out exhaustion. She stepped toward him, so close she could smell him. He didn't wear cologne, but she never forgot the smell of his musk. Before, his scent had been familiar and comforting before she began to associate it with nightmares.

"I did what I had to," she said through clenched teeth. "You don't get to judge me for that."

"Violet?"

She had been too focused on Jesse to notice Abel had pulled up to the curb. He had his windows down and was watching them intently.

"Abel," she said with false brightness and swallowed her rage. She got into the passenger seat and leaned over to kiss his cheek. "Thanks for picking me up."

"You didn't mention you were bringing anyone," Abel said as Jesse tossed their bags in the trunk.

"My stepbrother came to help."

Abel, ever courteous, turned in his seat to shake Jesse's hand. "I'm Abel."

"Jesse."

"I'm glad you're driving back to Texas with Vi. We were a little worried."

"I'm not driving to Alaska," she grumbled as she belted herself in.

"Still. You can get in trouble at a kid's birthday party," Abel said as he pulled into traffic. "It'll give us all peace of mind if you have someone to watch your back."

"What does that mean?" Jesse asked from the back seat.

She shot him a quelling look that he returned with a stoic one.

"You're her brother. You must know," Abel said with a grin. "She attracts the wrong kind of attention and always gets herself into trouble."

"Abel," she said in a repressive tone.

He laughed and patted her hand. "It's not your fault, Vi."

"No," she said with great restraint. "It isn't."

"Men won't leave her alone," Abel shared as he pulled

onto the interstate. "And she tends to put them down hard. Men don't take kindly to that."

Nothing from the back seat.

"By the way, Mason stopped by," Abel said with a sidelong glance.

"What for?"

"To get you back, I suppose. Reese told him you're moving. He wants you to call him."

"If I wanted to talk to him, I would have returned his calls." But that would be a difficult feat since she blocked him. "He didn't cause any trouble, did he?"

"Nah." His voice changed. "I'm sorry about your mom."

Just the thought of losing Lynne made her feel as if she couldn't breathe. She couldn't bear to talk about it. "Thanks. I need to leave as soon as possible."

"We figured that. We're going to help as much as we can." Abel's attention went to the rearview mirror. "I didn't know Vi had a brother. Do you live in Texas?"

"I'm in the Air Force," Jesse said.

Abel brightened. "My brother's in the Army."

She tuned them out as they made their way to her home for the past four years. Even though she knew moving to Texas was the right thing to do, she felt a niggle in her gut. Salt Lake City had given her a fresh slate. She made friends here and created a new life. This city helped her grow and heal... or so she thought.

*Did running away work?*

A wave of heat washed over her. She didn't run; she moved on with her life. Did he think she would wait around so when he came home on leave, she would be at his disposal? She had a life to live and wasn't going to waste any more of it wallowing on the past or him.

Listening to him and Abel put her on edge. She didn't

like Jesse encroaching on her life. This was hers. Here, he was nobody, and she wanted to keep it that way. Unfortunately, he and Abel seemed to be getting along swell. She strangled her seat belt as she listened to him extract information from Abel she wouldn't have provided—that she had originally dated Abel before she realized they didn't suit and introduced him to Reese. Abel filled him in on her brief college experience, some of her jobs, and was starting on her extensive dating life when she cut him off.

"That's enough," she snapped.

Abel grinned. "Don't want him to report back to your parents?"

No, she didn't want *him* to know. "You should be careful. You were at all those wild freshmen parties with me. I have a lot of ammunition for the speech I'm going to give at your wedding."

"Don't be so touchy, Vi. I'm talking to your brother, not your boyfriend."

She looked out the window. "Yeah, whatever. Let's not bore him with this shit. Have you guys set a date yet?"

"No."

When she caught the note of hesitancy in his voice, she turned to him. "What?"

He shrugged. "It might be delayed a little longer. We just put an offer on a house."

She straightened. "You did?"

"Yeah, and we got it." He shot her an uncertain look. "We've been thinking about it for a while. Reese wanted to wait, but it was too good a deal to pass up."

That explained the abrupt announcement that Reese wanted to move out, and Meg had agreed. As she had suspected, everyone was moving forward. She ignored the pang of regret in her chest and squeezed his forearm. "That's great news. I'm happy for you."

Abel shot her a quick glance. "You know, you don't have to move back to Texas if you don't want to. We can delay our move, or you can come to the new house with us. We're going to have lots of room—"

"You guys are so sweet, but I'm good," she said, even as a part of her considered the offer.

Life was still shoving her along too quickly for her to think. She had to make big, life-changing decisions on the spot. Was she in or out? It was tempting to stay when the city looked so pristine. It was a beautiful day with the mountains jutting toward the sky.

"Reese feels bad. She's going to try to convince you to stay," Abel said in a low voice. "And I know you need a job. I talked to my dad. Our receptionist is going on maternity leave, so you can see if that suits you."

"Abel." She was touched. "You know my track record and would still let me work at your family's company?"

"You're not a bad worker. You just haven't found the right job yet."

Her eyes stung with tears. Reese, Meg, and their men had become her support system. She was a fucking screw-up and forever dragging her drama along with her, but they never gave up on her. They were loyal and amazing and at that moment, she seriously reconsidered her move back to Texas. If she was here, she wouldn't have to see Jesse when he came home, but what about her father? An image of Lynne swam into focus, and her indecision died.

"I may take you up on it in the future, but right now, I need to go back. I think it's best."

Abel nodded. "Family is everything, but if it doesn't work out..."

"Yes." She rubbed his arm. "I'll be on your doorstep."

"I just want you to know you have somewhere to go," he said as he pulled up the driveway and killed the engine.

She leaned over and kissed his cheek. "Thank you."

Abel helped Jesse with the bags while she started toward the house. The door opened before she reached the front steps. Reese stood there in her business suit.

"What are you doing home? Aren't you supposed to be at work?" Violet asked as she approached.

"I got off early so I could be here." Reese gave her a tight hug. "Are you sure this is what you want, Vi?"

She returned the hug and rocked her from side to side. "Yes. Abel offered to let me live with you. You guys are the best."

Reese pulled away and searched her face. "You said no?"

"Yes, but I may come back to be your live-in nanny one day."

Reese blinked back tears. "I can't believe you're moving back to Texas."

"I know."

Reese's eyes moved past her and widened. "Hello."

Jesse put his hand on Violet's lower back. She stiffened and moved Reese over the threshold so they could all come inside.

"Well, *hiiii*," Reese drawled and gave her a pointed look. "I'm Reese, Violet's roommate."

He shook her limp hand. "Jesse."

Reese looked a bit dazed as her eyes moved over him.

"This is my stepbrother," she said, and Reese jolted. "He's here to help."

"Oh." Reese looked disappointed for a moment before she asked, "Lynne's your mom?" When he nodded, Reese's pretty face softened into sympathetic lines. "I'm so sorry."

"So am I," he said.

"Well." Reese clapped her hands together. "What do you want to do, Vi?"

"Might as well start now," Violet said and headed to her bedroom, which was the only one on the first floor.

"Let me change," Reese said and gave Abel a kiss before she headed upstairs. "Meg and Trent are coming this afternoon, and they're available tomorrow if you need them."

Violet nodded as she rounded the kitchen and approached her lair. She should have been prepared, but she wasn't. Her bedroom looked like it had been ransacked. Meg and Reese had emptied everything out of the drawers and closet so she could see what she had to pack.

Jesse came up beside her and examined the room for a moment before he asked, "What kind of car do you have?"

"A Jeep," she said faintly.

"You won't get much in there."

"I didn't think I had this much stuff."

"We may need to rent a truck if you want to take even a quarter of this stuff home."

She scrubbed her hands over her face and resisted the urge to turn around and walk out.

"All right!" Reese slipped past Jesse and held up both hands. "Don't freak out, okay? I have a system."

"Thank God."

As Reese explained the method to her madness, Jesse left the room. She heard the rumble of male voices in the kitchen and hoped Abel didn't disclose any more information about her. The less Jesse knew about her life post high school, the better.

With Reese's help, the room began to look less like it had been hit by a tornado and more as if she really was moving. They made piles for things to donate and what she wanted to take. It was clear she would have to rent a truck. That wouldn't be too expensive, right?

The guys made several trips to the Salvation Army, but it didn't seem to be clearing up the space. She kept unearthing things from under the bed.

"Maybe I shouldn't move," Violet said as she stared at the room, which looked worse than it had when they arrived.

"Tomorrow we'll pack what you want to take and figure out what size truck you'll need," Reese said as she brushed sweaty tendrils from her eyes. "Whatever you leave behind, Meg and I will take care of."

Thankfully, Meg and Trent arrived with food. Violet gave them quick hugs before she dug into the Chinese food and retreated to the living room, which had three couches around the fireplace. Everyone grabbed their plates and joined her. Most of the focus was on Jesse, no surprise. Her friends gave her odd looks but refrained from asking why she hadn't mentioned him in the past. Jesse was doing his impression of a well-mannered Southern man and honorable soldier.

Her stomach churned as she watched her friends fall under his spell. He would have excelled as a politician or businessman. If he was looking for a career outside the military, he could take his pick. His facade of open honesty made people trust him instinctively. She had, and it cost her everything. Listening to the familiar timbre of his voice made her want to curl up in a ball and cry. When she was seventeen, she experienced a betrayal so deep, she still hadn't recovered. He violated her love and trust for him, and it had tainted every relationship since.

Her friends offered funny stories about her, which only reinforced what a fuck up she'd become—her ever-changing jobs, failed relationships, and lack of direction. She inwardly groaned when Trent revealed that they met on the job and after a week of dating, she had introduced him to Meg. Even though she wanted to tell them all to shut up, the atmosphere was light and teasing, and they wouldn't understand why she wanted to keep this from Jesse. To them, this was harmless information, but for Jesse, it revealed how much he changed her. The cold, unaffected facade she wanted to project was in tatters. She felt the weight of his gaze but refused to look at him. She didn't want him here with her friends—good people who loved and supported her when she had no one. She wanted to hide beneath their protective wings, but it wasn't their job to care for her. She had wasted enough time, and Lynne was reminding her how short life truly was. She had to learn to stand on her own two feet and move forward.

"Is he for real?" Meg asked out of the side of her mouth.

"Really," Reese breathed and elbowed Violet, who was slouched between them. "Tell me there's something wrong with him."

She had a vivid memory of him pinning her down in the back of the SUV. "There's a lot wrong with him."

"Really?" Reese sounded intrigued.

Her heart sank. "Really."

"He's not married," Meg said, still speaking out of the corner of her mouth as Trent and Abel quizzed Jesse about the military.

"He must have a string of women at his beck and call," Reese said in low undertones. "Who wouldn't want him?"

Violet shot to her feet. "I'm going to shower."

"Of course," Meg said and leaned toward Reese. "He would have been perfect for Janelle."

"Yes, oh my God, you're so right!"

Violet stalked into her demolished bedroom and dug through her duffel for clothes before she headed to the bathroom. She filled the tub and tossed in all the bath salts she had been saving for a special occasion and lit the ocean breeze candle that had been sitting on her toilet tank for two years. The clash of aromas soothed her. She swished her foot in the water to dissolve the last of the salts before she submerged herself. Heat penetrated her bones and melted her tension.

Tomorrow they would pack and rent a truck. That possibility hadn't crossed her mind, but maybe that was a good thing. Jesse could drive the truck, and she would follow in her Jeep. That way, she could still get her alone time and converse with him only when they had to refuel. How much would that cost? Her hands flexed beneath the water as she tried to suppress her financial worries. These were her last expenses. Once she moved home, everything would be okay.

The sound of laughter drifting from the living room made her blood pressure rise. She didn't want them to like Jesse, but it was obvious they did. No one would believe what he was capable of. Even though she was the victim of his sick fantasies, a part of her still wanted to believe it was all some misunderstanding, but she knew better. He really fucked her. Fucked her so many times that she couldn't keep count. He forced himself on her every chance he got. He never showed any remorse for his actions, either. Even now... *Did running away work?* She slapped the surface of the water, sending a mini wave sloshing out of the tub. He was such a fucker!

She raised both hands and made Zen fingers—pointer and thumb creating a circle with her palms up. She listened to her candle sputter for a second before it quieted. She closed her eyes and tried to zone out. More laughter rang out. Her breathing quickened. She forced it to even out. She tried to blank her mind, but flashbacks rose to choke her. She erupted from the tub, unable to stay still or gain any semblance of tranquility.

By the time she emerged from the bathroom, the house was quiet. She tiptoed toward the living room and saw Jesse sitting on the couch with his phone. His face, illuminated by his screen, lifted when she stopped.

"I'll get you some pillows," she said.

"Reese brought me some."

Of course, she did. She lifted her hand in a stiff, awkward wave. "See you tomorrow."

She walked into her bedroom and locked the door as she dialed Lynne's phone. "Hey, Mom. How are you?"

"Great! Jesse just called and said your friends are so nice."

She gave the room a tight smile. "Yes, they're the best."

"He said you'll probably head out the day after tomorrow."

That's what she had planned, but she didn't like that he was calling the shots. This was *her* move, not his.

"I can't wait for y'all to come back. Dad and I went out today. I bought a new bathing suit. It's yellow, my favorite color! I got you one too. It's this lovely fuchsia that will look great on you. I'm looking forward to lying on the beach."

"Me too," she said as she sank onto the edge of the bed.

"Dad's happy you're moving home," Lynne said quietly. "He's missed you, and you didn't visit that much."

"Well, I'm about to make up for my absence."

"You're a good girl, dropping everything to come home."

She blinked hastily. "You're my family. I'd do

anything..." Her voice broke, and she clapped a hand over her mouth, but it was too late.

"Vi," Lynne cooed, which made Violet keel over as something twisted in her chest. "Don't cry. This is the beginning of something great, a new beginning for all of us."

She shook her head with her hand over her mouth to hold back her sobs. She didn't want anything to change. She needed everything to stay just like this.

"We have to accept God's will for our lives."

Violet immediately rejected that sentiment. God had abandoned her long ago. "Everything is happening too fast," she rasped.

"That's when you know God is taking over and carving out the right path for you."

Both of her parents were devout Christians. She had no idea how they would handle the truth about Jesse. Would they sweep it under the rug? Pray for him and think that would cure him? Would they call her a liar? She shook those thoughts away. "I'm beat."

"I'm sure you are. It's been a rough week for you. Get some rest and I want to hear your progress tomorrow."

"Will do. I love you."

"I love you more. God bless."

Violet dropped back on the bed, crossed her arms over her chest, and wept.

# CHAPTER 5



"Ma'am, your card's been declined."

Violet's fingers tingled with cold panic. "Are you sure?"

"I tried twice. Is there another card we can use?"

She fumbled in her wallet as her mind raced. "Can we divide the total between three cards?"

"Here." Jesse extended his card. "Put it on this."

She closed her eyes as mortification consumed her. "Thank you," she said hoarsely.

"No problem," he said easily.

"You have a stand-up guy," the man across the counter said with a wink. "I think you better keep this one."

She opened her mouth to say something, but nothing came out.

"Add the trailer too," Jesse said.

When she glanced at him, she found him watching her.

"We don't want to get separated," he said.

"Of course, you don't," the worker said jovially and added the trailer she had nixed to their total. "So, we're doing a twenty-foot moving truck with a trailer to transport your car. Nice."

Jesse took over as she sat frozen in her seat. The men went over the contract and in short order, Jesse had a set of keys in hand. When he and the employee went outside to look over the truck and trailer, she ambled in their wake, arms crossed over her chest.

The day had been progressing nicely. She woke early and with Meg, Trent, and Jesse's help, they were able to get everything sorted and packed. She was taking more shit home than she had ever dreamed, but she told herself it was worth it until she heard how much it would cost to rent the truck. She was indebted to Jesse, the last person on the planet she wanted to feel gratitude toward.

When Jesse waved her over, she climbed into the passenger seat. He made some minor adjustments to his seat before he drove off the lot.

"Thank you," she said again, staring straight ahead.

"Don't worry about it."

"I'll pay you back."

"I said, don't worry about it."

She clasped her hands in her lap. "I think I can still drive even with a trailer on the back. It shouldn't be too hard, right? I mean, especially on the long stretches. I think we should take turns. I don't want you to—"

"You're rambling."

She glanced at him as he navigated the city with ease, thanks to his GPS. He looked so competent, while her image of a mature adult was in tatters. He got a front-row ticket to the mess she had made of her life while he was still standing tall. She was so frustrated, she wanted to cry, but she'd be damned if she showed any more weakness.

"You want to talk about it?" he asked.

"No," she said through clenched teeth.

The cab was uncomfortably intimate. Knowing they

would spend almost twenty-four hours in the small space made her palms sweat.

When they pulled up to the house, Trent came outside to help disconnect the trailer so they could load the truck. When they finished, Trent drove her Jeep onto the trailer. As the sun set, Jesse parked the loaded moving truck on the street so they could leave bright and early tomorrow. Reese pulled up as Jesse hopped out of the cab. Reese looked from the truck to Violet and fanned her face as her eyes filled with tears.

"I can't believe you're leaving!"

"I know. I can't believe it myself."

They walked into the house with their arms around each other.

"You know you have to visit regularly," Reese said.

"I will."

Reese pushed her toward the bathroom. "Get dressed. We're going out."

They piled into Abel's SUV and headed to her favorite Mexican restaurant. Trent took his car since Meg was spending the night at his place. As soon as they were seated, she ordered a margarita. Meg and Reese ordered sangria's while the guys ordered beers. The girls didn't need to look at the menu. They got a variety of dishes they were going to share. This restaurant was their go-to for celebrations, breakups, and pick-me-ups. After the week she'd had, she was looking forward to good food and company... Minus Jesse.

She spent most of the meal ignoring him and trying to cram in as much quality time with her friends as possible. The more drinks they slugged back, the more emotional they became until Jesse put a stop to it.

"She's done," he told the waiter.

"He's a kill joy," Violet said in a loud whisper to her friends.

"You're going to feel like shit on the road tomorrow."

She scowled at him. "I can handle it."

"I don't feel like stopping so you can throw up on the side of the road."

"He's right," Reese said and slid a glass of water in front of her. "You have a long drive ahead of you."

Which is why she wanted to be shit-faced. That long ass drive in a confined space with him? Hell no. Despite Jesse's interference, she was feeling pleasantly fuzzy as she said a tearful goodbye to Meg and Trent. Apparently, Jesse hadn't been watching Abel as closely as he'd been watching her. Abel and Reese were tipsy and leaning on each other for support when they left, which made him the designated driver.

She must have fallen asleep during the drive because she woke draped over Jesse's shoulder. She thumped his buns of steel.

"Can walk," she groaned and began to giggle. Everything looked so weird upside down.

Her world spun as he settled her on the bed. She clutched the covers because her head was spinning.

"Oh, God."

"You're plastered," he said as he slipped off her shoes.

She grunted and closed her eyes. She felt like she was on a rocking ship, which was quite pleasant. She was about to drift off when her body jerked.

"What the—?"

"You need your jeans off."

"Why?" she grouched.

He didn't answer. He pulled them off and then unbuttoned her wrinkled blouse.

"What doing?" she huffed and batted at him.

He rubbed her belly with a calloused hand. She smiled and lazily kicked her feet, which dangled over the side of the bed.

"Feel good?" he murmured.

"Umm hmm."

"I'll make you feel even better."

He brushed sweet kisses over her face. She didn't fight. She lay there with her arms spread wide as he soothed her with comforting strokes over her bare skin. She felt a whoosh of air as he sank to his knees beside the bed and pulled on her heavy body until her butt rested on the edge. He kissed her knees before he parted them.

"Tickles," she mumbled.

When he did it again, her toes bumped against his abs. What happened to his clothes? He braced her feet on his stomach and massaged her calves, kneading the tense muscles. She moaned. Ooh, that felt nice. When his lips brushed over her inner thighs, her toes curled.

"Who am I?"

His voice seemed to bounce off the walls. She jolted.

"Why are you yelling?"

"I'm not yelling. I need to know you're with me, Vi. Who am I?"

"Fucking boogieman," she said as she plucked at the quilt beneath her.

"What?"

"Mr. Perfect. No one knows the real you."

He rose over her and planted his hands on either side of her head. The streetlights coming in through the blinds gave him strange orange stripes. He looked evil, dark, otherworldly.

"Monster," she said and placed a hand on his bare chest.

He gripped her chin. "My name, Vi." When she stared at him, he pressed a kiss to her parted lips. "Foolish girl. Drinking leaves you defenseless." His finger traced her jaw and then the line of her throat. "You should take better care."

He nibbled on her lips while his hands shaped her body. He pressed his groin against hers and let out a soft groan.

"I jerked off with the underwear you left in the bathroom last night. I didn't want to do that tonight, and you gave me the perfect opening."

His next kiss was so deep, he stole her breath. She clutched at him as he ground himself against her. When she arched, he broke the kiss.

"I'm gonna come on your fucking leg," he hissed as he gripped her hair and pulled. "Say my fucking name."

"Jesse."

He pressed his forehead to hers. "Yes. Jesse. That's the only name that should be on your lips."

His hand played with the waistband of her underwear before slipping beneath. Thick fingers parted her folds and then slipped inside her. She closed her eyes and hummed as she enjoyed the fire heating her blood.

"Beautiful," he breathed as he kissed her collarbone. "You were made for me."

His weight and heat disappeared. Her eyelids fluttered as firm hands folded her legs up and pinned her knees to her chest. This position wasn't comfortable. She was trying to gather the energy to move when she felt something part her folds. It took less than five seconds for her to be okay with her legs being pressed to her abdomen. Nothing mattered except that tongue dancing over her. Her blood fizzled in her veins. As pleasure built, her hands moved restlessly over the covers, herself, and then found anchor by gripping handfuls of sweat soaked hair. Her breath hitched as that talented mouth worked her into a frenzy. She trembled like a plucked string.

"Jesse."

The mouth disappeared. Before she could cry out in disappointment, a large body covered hers. A thick penis intruded, stretching her unbearably. She grunted, and a mouth covered hers as he began to thrust, fucking her on the edge of the bed where it was firmer so he could go deeper. When she orgasmed, she screamed into his mouth. He gave her his groan as he shoved deep and came.

# CHAPTER 6

Her rage was ice-cold. It didn't matter that her head was pounding, her mouth was dry, and despite drinking water and coffee, she could still taste tequila on her tongue. The cloudy day matched her dark mood. Jesse woke her at the crack of dawn. He was dressed and ready to go while she was naked, hungover, and dirty. There was a moment of disorientation as she stared at him, a hand wrapped in his shirt as she tried to think.

"A shower will help," he said as he brushed her hair back from her face.

She grimaced and ran a hand over her aching body. "What?" She had a fuzzy recollection of their drunken fuck. She stiffened. "Did you...?"

"We," he confirmed as he brushed a kiss over her lips. "Come on, let's go."

She erupted from the bed and shoved him. "Damn it, Jesse! How could you?"

"Easily," he said without a shade of remorse. "Shower, get dressed. We leave in twenty minutes. We have a long day ahead of us."

He left her standing in the middle of the empty room, staring after him.

She didn't understand him. He knew she hated him for it, yet he continued to push and use her for sex every chance he got. Was he a sex addict? A sociopath? A rapist who got off on her resistance? One moment he was helpful, generous, caring. The next, he was intent on sating himself no matter the cost. Lynne's impending death hadn't affected his libido. He was as forceful and ravenous as he had been five years ago, maybe even more so.

Why?

She woke Reese and Abel to say her goodbye and was pissed when Jesse made an appearance and thanked them for their hospitality. His ability to fool everyone infuriated her. She was incredulous when Abel extended an invitation to Jesse to attend their wedding. She hoped Abel was just being nice and not serious. These were *her* friends, not his. If Abel and Reese hadn't been drunk and gone upstairs, would he have made a move? Who was she kidding? Even if their rooms were side by side, Jesse dared. What the fuck was wrong with him?

Not one word was said between them as they headed out of Salt Lake City. The only sound in the cab came from the robotic female voice on the GPS giving them directions and the radio playing classic country tunes.

She should sleep, since she couldn't have gotten more than a few hours, but she was too angry. Hazy images from last night kept slipping through her mind. He had been gentle with her. He aroused her with petting and sweet kisses before he took her. To her, this was worse than the other times because it was a complete farce. He took advantage of her inebriated state to bend her to his will. Her blood curdled with resentment and shame.

Hours passed. Jesse didn't seem bothered by the silence. On the contrary, he acted as if she wasn't present, which pissed her off even more. He hummed along with the radio and drove hour after hour without complaint. He acted as if road trips weren't out of the ordinary for him. To her knowledge, this was the first time he had ever done such a thing. Once again, he was showing his adaptability while she scrambled to keep up.

She updated her friends and parents on their progress through text and during their first rest stop, received a voicemail from Planned Parenthood who said the STD test was negative. That was one small piece of good news. Every time they stopped for fuel, she used the facilities and took the time to stretch her legs. He didn't ask her to pay, so she didn't offer to. She didn't feel like she owed him anymore. Apparently, he thought her body was his to use whenever he felt like it, so if he wanted to pick up the tab for this move, she would let him. She waited until the last possible second before she reluctantly climbed back into the truck with him.

They crossed into Colorado and then New Mexico. By one in the afternoon, she was over it. Traveling on the road had a very similar feel to flying in an airplane. She was dehydrated, exhausted, and felt dirty even though she had done nothing more strenuous than sit. She had seriously underestimated how taxing this move would be financially, emotionally, and physically. She tried to sleep, but it was impossible with every fiber of her being focused on the devil sitting within touching distance.

He was too close for comfort. The cab had two captain's chairs with a space in between where they had their bags and a small cooler. Directly behind their chairs was a wall. Thankfully, the windshield was massive and gave the illusion of space, but the confines were stifling. He was slightly slouched in his seat, completely relaxed, with one hand on the steering wheel. He was in his customary jeans, white shirt, and boots. It annoyed her that no matter the setting, he looked as if he belonged there. Asshole.

She couldn't take in the landscape, not when memories she thought she erased rose to taunt her. For years, she had kept everything bottled up, but he roused everything to a fever pitch. When she moved to Utah, she kept busy with school, partying, men, shopping—anything to keep herself from dwelling on what happened between them. Time had done it's work and made the memories easier to bear, but his reappearance brought them back to the fore. She wanted to weep, rage, attack. Instead, she sat there with her hands in her lap, staring straight ahead, while everything in her revolted to being in his presence.

"You're lucky you found such good friends in Salt Lake City."

His voice, so unexpected after hours of silence, made her jump. She shot him a lethal glare before she returned her attention to the road. She knew she was fortunate. She didn't need him to tell her that.

"You've been busy."

Something about his casual tone made her tense.

"Lots of jobs," he said as he tapped a finger on the steering wheel.

His attempt at making conversation was fucking lousy.

"Lots of men, too."

She sucked in a breath, but the sound was drowned out by traffic and the truck as it rattled down the interstate.

"Did it work?" he asked.

"Work?" The word left her mouth before she could stop herself.

He glanced at her, but she couldn't see his eyes since they were covered by dark shades.

"You fucked them to forget about me. Did it work?"

Her mouth dropped open. "You conceited son of a bitch!"

"Mom would be hurt if she heard you say that," he said mildly.

"You're the biggest narcissist I've ever met!"

"If I have nothing to do with your body count, then what's your explanation for the man parade your friends talked about?"

She leaned toward him so far, her seat belt locked. "I wanted, so I took. That should sound familiar to you!"

He didn't look at her as he continued in that placid tone that made her want to hit him.

"Seems no one measured up. None of them lasted longer than a few months."

"I have high standards!"

"Doesn't sound like it. I heard one of the guys you dated a few months ago worked at a video game store."

"Justin was sweet!"

"It's *Dustin*, actually," he said coolly. "Seems he wasn't sweet enough for you to remember his name."

"His name *is* Justin!" It was, right?

He shrugged. "You should know."

"Yes, I *do* know. What I do and who I do it with is none of your fucking business!"

He shook his head. "We've been over this before."

*Everything you do is my business.*

"I'm a big girl. I can take care of myself."

"Debatable. It sounds like your friends have been carrying you for a while now."

She felt as if she had been kicked in the gut. "You don't know anything about my life."

"You dropped out of school, can't keep a job, and bang anyone who catches your eye. Am I missing anything?"

He had turned into Mr. Hyde again. Now that they were alone, he had morphed back into the monster she brought out in him with little effort. His succinct and brutal summary of her life made her flush.

"You haven't changed. You're still dating losers because you don't want it to go anywhere, and you want to be in control. The few times you ran into good guys, you gave them to your friends or walked away. You took what you wanted before you got bored and moved onto the next schmuck."

"Stop," she said faintly.

"Empty fucks." The tendons in his arm flexed as he gripped the steering wheel. "I know exactly how that feels. I took every woman who offered."

He was no longer slouched in his seat. He was sitting up straight, body radiating with tension. He was driving a little faster than he'd been a minute ago. The unruffled veneer he had maintained throughout the day was beginning to shred.

"Did sleeping with all those men help you forget about me, or did it make you realize nothing comes close to what's between us?" he challenged.

"Shut up!"

"Last night, you gave yourself to me."

"I was *drunk*! You took advantage of that."

"When your guard is down, you show your true feelings."

"True feelings?" she echoed in a strangled voice. "My

true feeling is that I hate you! *Loathe* you. If I never saw you again, I—"

"You begged me to never leave you."

He conjured up memories too painful to revisit. "Stop."

"You said we were a unit."

She shrank in her seat and stared straight ahead. "That was a long time ago."

"Feels like yesterday to me."

"That was before…"

"Before I caught Tucker with his hand in your shorts?"

"We're not talking about that!"

Her hands were clammy with panic. He was bringing it all back—her worst memories and the moment everything changed. She searched for an exit, but there was none. She was locked in this suffocating cab with a man intent on emotionally stripping her.

She could still remember Tucker being ripped away from her and the look on Jesse's face as he pinned Tucker to the pavement and beat the shit out of him. It sent a chill down her spine. He could have killed him. If she hadn't thrown herself at Jesse, who knew how far he would have gone? Jesse drove her home, and… She shut her eyes against the memories bombarding her. That was the day her world turned gray.

"You haven't changed. You're still throwing yourself away on men who will never satisfy you."

"You think you're the only one who can get me off? You're delusional. You're lucky I remember your name. You're just another dick to me. Nothing special."

He turned his head and stared at her for so long that she reached for the wheel.

"Jesse!"

When he returned his gaze to the road, the cab was

once again enfolded in silence, but this time the tension was so thick she couldn't breathe. She watched him out of the corner of her eye, waiting for him to lash out or explode. He did neither. He slowed his speed to match the other cars, sat back, and resumed the journey as if nothing had happened. The fact that he could swallow up his emotions like that unnerved her.

She tried to mimic his unruffled poise. It took every ounce of control she had not to rail at him as he deserved. He got her worked up and then switched off again while she was at the boiling point. Who was he to judge her choices? She turned her face away so he wouldn't see her furious tears.

By the time they covered another hundred miles, most of her rage had seeped out of her, leaving her drained and wishing this was over. Crazy ideas passed through her head of catching a flight home, but they were in the middle of nowhere and their parents would know something was wrong. Mom assumed they were having quality bonding time. If she only knew... Lynne sent a steady stream of images from the Florida resort they would be staying at. Knowing every minute brought them closer to Austin kept Violet sane. She could handle this. Just another thirteen hours...

She had sunken into a glum daze when Jesse cursed and lurched forward. She jolted and watched as he messed with his phone. She glanced at him, the road, and back.

"What's going on?" she asked warily, ready to make another grab for the wheel.

"I should have stopped at the last gas station. I thought we'd make it to the next town, but I don't think we can. I need to refuel quick."

"Here." She held out her hand and was relieved when he

handed the phone to her. It took her a few seconds to figure out how to find the nearest gas station. "In ten miles, take the exit."

She held his phone and fed him directions. She couldn't see the gas gauge from where she was sitting, but if he was worried, it must be alarmingly low. Because they were towing the trailer, the truck needed to be fueled frequently. Every time they filled the tank, it cost around one hundred and fifty dollars. She wouldn't have been able to make it halfway home before her credit card maxed out.

They were the only vehicle to take the exit. They were in the middle of nowhere. There were no signs for a town, just a lone service station that couldn't be seen from the interstate. It was late in the afternoon and her non-existent energy was at an all-time low. She hoped this gas station had a store with sugary goodies in it. That hope died quickly when she saw not one vehicle at the four available pumps.

"Is this place abandoned?" she asked.

"I hope not. We're not going to make it far if it is."

As he hopped out, she set his phone in the cradle and paused when she saw a message flash across the screen.

*Tanya: I miss you.*

She felt an odd dipping sensation in her stomach. He told her he wasn't fucking anyone else, but he was a compulsive liar. She couldn't believe a damn thing he said. But at least he didn't have any STDs. He could play with whomever he wanted. Maybe she would push Marissa on him once they got home. He could fuck her for the duration of his leave.

As she slid out of the truck, she raised a hand to block her eyes from the hot breeze that blew sand and dirt everywhere. She watched as he stuck his card in the machine and was relieved when the screen lit up and beeped.

"I'm gonna check it out," she said without meeting his eyes.

She spotted bathrooms off to the left but walked into the tiny store first. There was no one behind the counter and all they had to offer was one case of assorted sodas, a smattering of candy bars that were faded with age, and corned nuts. She exited as quickly as she came in. She wasn't looking forward to the state of the restrooms, but she had to take what she could get. Who knew when they'd stop again?

There were old beer bottles and trash scattered around, and some trucks parked in the distance. Presumably, the drivers were taking a nap. Odd place to stop.

Despite how small the station was, there were separate male and female bathrooms and when she pushed the door open to the women's side, she found two stalls. They were covered in graffiti and there was no light aside from the sun streaming through the wooden louvers high up on the wall. Only one of the stalls had a door, but there was no lock. Of course, it didn't. She was relieved to see toilet paper and vowed that on her next road trip she was going to bring several rolls with her. She squatted over the toilet, sure her ass would break out in a rash if she made contact with that nasty seat. This place was hella creepy. She wanted to get the hell out of here as soon as possible.

She had just finished washing her hands when the door opened behind her. In the cracked, dingy mirror, she saw Jesse standing there. She whirled around with dripping hands.

"What's wrong?" she asked, ready to run, sure he was about to tell her some crazy shit was going down outside.

She blinked when he stepped in, letting the door swing shut, once again enclosing her in semi-darkness.

"What—?" she began, but her voice died when she heard the snick of the lock being turned.

He stood in the shadows, not saying a thing. Her heartbeat accelerated. She took a step back and bumped into the sink.

"Jesse?"

He erupted from the darkness. Hard hands gripped her shoulders and shoved her against the grimy tiles. Her scream was cut off by a large hand clamping over her mouth.

*"Don't."* His voice shook with rage. "You think you can say I'm just another dick, and I'll let that pass?"

She moaned into his hand. Oh, God. He had been stewing over this for the past hour?

He unbuttoned her jeans and shoved his hand in her pants, easily bypassing her silky underwear and sinking his blunt middle finger into her. She gasped, jumped, and thumped his chest with her fists, but he was an immovable brick wall in front of her. Outside, the wind picked up, making the louvers sing.

"You want me to be just another dick to you, but I'm not. You're in my blood, just as I'm in yours. Those men you threw yourself away on didn't last long because they weren't me."

She went on her tiptoes as he slipped another finger in her and applied pressure on her G spot. She shrieked and shoved at him, but he leaned into her, making anything she did with her hands ineffective. She was at his mercy. He smelled of sweat and himself. It was so familiar, a smell she associated with her childhood and the good old days before he tainted those memories with debauchery.

"I claimed you at seventeen," he said harshly. "I took your virginity and imprinted myself on you. You'll never be free of me."

She tried to shake her head, but she couldn't with his hand pinning her to the tiles. She wasn't sure if it was fear or her body reacting instinctively to his intrusion, but her body secreted, coating his fingers in natural lube. He dropped his face into her hair and groaned.

"You feel that, baby? Your body yearns for mine. How can you deny what's between us? You were made for me, Violet. Why won't you admit it?"

"*Noph!*"

Her denial came out garbled, but he apparently understood because he tensed. He lifted his head and examined her face, illuminated by slivers of sunlight, while his was cast in shadow.

"You fight me, but you fight yourself harder," he murmured.

His fingers began to caress. Fear morphed into pleasure. She clawed his wrist, but he didn't let up.

"You're so worried about what people will say that you would deprive us both."

He did something with his fingers that made her whimper.

"I'm not so self-sacrificing. I suffered, Vi. Five years without you. I can't do it anymore. I'm taking my fill."

He scissored his fingers, making her jerk like a puppet on a string.

"You're trying to be a good Christian girl, but you like it rough and dirty. How can anything that feels so good be a sin? Feel me. Yes. You like that, don't you? I remember everything that makes you tick. I taught you to crave me."

She gripped his wrist with both hands and rocked her

hips before she caught herself and stilled. She saw the glint of white as he smiled.

"That's my girl."

Abruptly, his hand disappeared from between her legs. He pressed a hand against her chest to brace her against the wall as he dragged her pants down. She widened her stance to stop him from pulling them off completely. He tipped her off balance and roughly yanked her jeans off one ankle before he turned and shuffled her toward the sink.

"Jesse!"

Her voice echoed loudly around the restroom and traveled easily now that the wind had died down, but that didn't stop him. She heard the hiss of his zipper before he bent her over with a hand on her back, flattening her against the sink. She gripped both sides of the grimy porcelain and opened her mouth to shout, but she wasn't paying attention to what he was doing. He slammed into her with such force, she nearly crashed into the mirror. She yelped and slapped a hand on the dusty surface as he let loose.

She didn't have the breath to call for help, not when he was fucking her so hard, she could barely think straight. It was no holds barred. He gripped her hair and yanked her head to the side as he scraped his teeth on her shoulder and then bit down. His other hand coasted down her front before he grabbed her breast and pinched her nipple. She screamed and bucked as he lapped at his bite and then moved to her ear lobe and bit again.

"*Stop!*"

The hand on her breast went to her mouth and squeezed so hard, she panicked and clawed at him. His grip eased enough for her to breathe. One hand splayed on the mirror as he fucked her. Their reflection was alarming—a large, clothed man demanding submission from a smaller form. Her nipples stood at attention while her shirt rode up because of the veined arm wrapped around her middle, holding her in place. Her gaze collided with his. He was watching her. His eyes seemed to glow with manic, animal lust. She closed her eyes and tried to shut off her mind and distance herself from what was happening. Her eyes flew open as he pulled out, spun her, and pushed her back against the wall. He hefted her up and slid into her as she tried to get her bearings.

She wasn't prepared for his tongue to steal into her mouth. He tasted of the grape Gatorade he had been nursing from their last pit stop. He let out a low groan as he rocked against her. She could feel him vibrating against her, trying to hold himself back. For what?

He kissed her cheek, the bite on her shoulder, and sucked on her neck before he came back to her parted lips. She couldn't comprehend what was happening, so she lay there pliant, body throbbing, mind in shambles.

"I need you with me," he whispered.

She tried to turn her face away, but his hand held her still as he assaulted her mouth. He stole her breath and gave her his. It was carnal and tinged with desperation. He stirred up emotions she didn't understand or want to feel. Her nails sank into his chest as his other slid down and touched her clit. Oh, shit. She let out a mewl of angry plea-sure and felt his lips curve against hers. When she fought him, he focused on keeping her mouth busy, a double assault that short-circuited her brain. The orgasm caught her off guard. One moment she was fine and the next, she exploded, bucking forward, nearly unseating him. He growled as he fought her back against the tiles and thrust, making her orgasm painfully pleasurable. As she spasmed, he buried his face in her hair and roared, pounding her ass into the wall as he came.

Her ears rang as she came down from the high. She was aware of his hot breath fanning her cheek and the wind that began to pick up again. Her legs, which had wrapped around his waist at some point, dropped heavily to the ground. His hand skated over her throbbing ass and gripped, pulling her more firmly against him. When she moaned, he hummed contentedly. His calloused hand stroked her hip as he pulled out of her. She sucked in a breath as his hand slid inside her, bathing his fingers in his cum and spreading it over her belly as he rested his forehead against hers.

"I'm capable of anything when it comes to you," he said in a low, gravelly voice. "But you already know that. Don't push me."

She stared at him. She didn't know what to say or how to feel. He must not have liked her expression because the hand coated in cum came to her face. His stained fingers drifted over her lips. When she opened her mouth to protest, he slipped them in her mouth.

"Taste us," he ordered.

Her mouth watered as his fingers stroked her tongue.

"Suck."

She had no choice but to swallow or let her saliva dribble out of her mouth. When his hand threatened to sink deeper, she gripped his wrist and dutifully suckled.

"As the years passed, I convinced myself that you couldn't be what I remembered," he said hoarsely. "That what you roused in me was a mad adolescent obsession, and I'd be over it by now."

He retracted his fingers from her mouth and held her still as he sampled her lips and sent his tongue into her moist cavern. His tongue explored with aching slowness. Her breathing was ragged when he pulled away. He stared at her for a long minute. She waited.

"I never got over it," he said quietly.

She shivered as his fingers traveled down to her breast and cupped her with a tenderness he hadn't shown a minute ago. She braced her hand on his chest.

"Stop," she whispered. She didn't want him petting to make up for what just happened between them.

His hand massaged as his head dipped down. He latched their lips together, even as she pushed for space and tried to sidle away. A hand on her hip kept her where he wanted her. He kissed her with such absorption, she started trembling. He made a noise in the back of his throat and stroked her back as he gentled the kiss.

"Maybe I deserve to burn in hell for what I've done," he said against her lips, "but it'll be worth it."

When he stepped back, her legs nearly gave out. He steadied her before he moved to the stall without a door. She slumped against the tiles and stared at the windows and the flickering light as clouds passed overhead. The wind was raging again. Dust drifted over her bare legs. She stumbled to the sink and washed her face, pieces of her hair, and scooped what she could of him out of her. She used her underwear to pat herself dry since there were no paper towels and pulled up her jeans.

Jesse came up to the sink beside her. She turned away and strode for the door. She unlocked it and burst through, desperate for air and precious seconds without his stifling presence.

Out of the corner of her eye, she saw an old man sitting in front of the store smoking a pipe. He hadn't been there earlier. She skidded to a stop and stared at him before she felt a hand on her lower back.

"Let's get out of here," Jesse said.

She smacked his hand away and marched toward the truck. "Don't touch me."

She stood outside the passenger door as he climbed in from the opposite side. The truck rumbled when he turned the key. She waited until the last possible second before she climbed in. He didn't say a word as they pulled away from the service station. She glanced at the GPS and felt her eyes burn with tears. They had eight hundred miles to go, which would take another twelve hours. Their estimated time of arrival in Austin was four in the morning. She wanted to give up already. Fuck all her stuff. Leave it in the middle of the desert. Nothing was worth this.

Her head throbbed with an oncoming migraine. Not a surprise when she was stressed, had no sleep, and was being physically and emotionally fucked by her step-brother. She fumbled through her purse and said a silent prayer of thanks when she found aspirin. It would take the edge off. She shook out two pills and gulped down water before she huddled against the door and prayed that God would save her from this hell.

She couldn't wrap her mind around what happened in that restroom. Or last night. Or the other times he forced her since he had come home. She felt just as lost, dazed, and shell-shocked as she had when he turned the tables on her when she was seventeen. One day, he was her brother and the next he was a stranger. There were long stretches of time when everything seemed normal. So much so, she wondered if she was going crazy and doubted her sanity until it happened again. And again. And again. Her junior year of high school, she felt like she was walking on a tightrope. One misstep and her world would crumble. It was happening all over again. No matter how much time passed, no matter how much she fortified her walls, he would lay siege. And he would win. He didn't recognize any barriers, which made him dangerous and terrifying.

A tear trickled out of the corner of her eye. She didn't understand him or what drove him to do the things he did, but he had dragged her under with him and she couldn't see the light. He forced her to partake in his salacious fantasies, and she would never be the same. He was right. She liked it rough and dirty. None of the men she dated could give her what she needed. None of them came close and when she nudged them towards the dark pool she wanted them to swim in, they backed away after dipping a toe in the water.

Jesse changed her, and she hated the person she had become. She was afraid to let anyone close because she didn't want them to see who she really was. Ever since him, she hadn't felt right. Nothing assuaged the restlessness within her. She wanted routine and stability yet continually acted on rash impulses. She wanted to be around her friends and yet, when she was in a crowd, perversely wished she were alone. She was never satisfied and constantly craving something she couldn't define.

Her vision blurred as she stared out the window at the passing scenery. She was in line with the vent that blew out icy air and turned her face numb. Good. If only the air conditioning had the same effect on her emotions. She would rather feel nothing than have her insides churn and riot. There was only one escape open to her, so she took it. She closed her eyes and tried to take refuge in sleep.

# CHAPTER 7

EIGHT YEARS AGO

SHE KNOCKED ON THE DOOR LEADING INTO JESSE'S ROOM FROM the bathroom. She cracked it open and saw him sitting up in bed with a book. He frowned at her, but she ignored that and hopped onto his bed.

"They're fighting again," she said miserably.

"I noticed."

"I hate it."

"It'll blow over."

She leaned into him as the shouting got louder. "What if they break up?"

"They won't."

Jesse didn't sound concerned in the least.

"How can you be so sure?"

"My parents used to fight all the time."

"But don't they love each other?" She twisted the ends of her shirt, a habit Lynne hated because it stretched out all her clothes.

"People who love each other can still fight."

"*We* don't fight!"

His brows shot up. "Didn't we fight two days ago at the movie theater?"

She scowled. "You wanted to watch a war movie, and we don't fight like *that*."

She jabbed her finger at the door. Even though their parent's room was down the hall, and the door was closed, she could hear every word being said. It wasn't pretty. They were arguing about money. Lynne and Dad rarely fought, but when they did, it felt like World War III.

Jesse shrugged. "Fighting isn't bad. It gets your feelings out."

She shuddered. "I hate it."

"It'll pass."

"It's been going on for half an hour." She flinched when she heard something crash. "Why does she *do* that?"

"She wants a reaction out of him," Jesse said mildly as he turned the page.

Desperate for a distraction, she peeked at his book. "What are you reading?"

"It's about a sniper."

She made a face. "You aren't really going into the military, are you?"

His eyes moved from the book to her. "You know, I promised my dad I would enlist."

"What about *me*?"

"What about you?"

Her eyes bugged. "You're going to leave me?"

"Mom and Dad are here."

"But we do everything together. What am I going to do without you?"

His eyes moved over her upturned face. She didn't know what he was thinking, but he put his arm around her and tucked her close. She closed her eyes and breathed in his scent. He always smelled nice. Her friends thought he was a hottie. She liked his face, but she didn't allow herself to look deeper than that. Jesse was Jesse.

The fight continued, but she found she could handle it now that she was weathering the storm with her brother. He played with her hair as he read, which had a drugging effect on her. When she slumped against him, he told her to stretch out. She did so and tucked her face against his thigh. His hand returned to her hair, and she fell asleep, knowing that everything was going to be okay.

She roused slightly when she heard, "Jesse?"

"Shh, she's asleep."

Soft footsteps and then, "Why's she in here?"

"You know she freaks out when you two fight."

"Sorry. Here, let me take her."

"She's fine."

"Are you sure?"

"Yeah."

She heard Lynne kiss his cheek. "You're such a good big brother."

"Did you two settle your issues?" Jesse asked.

"Yes. I'm sorry you had to hear that."

"I'm fine, but next time, give me a heads-up, so I can take her out before you start breaking things."

"I'll do that. Isaac's the opposite of your father. He doesn't tell me how he feels and shuts down instead of talking to me. It takes drastic measures to make him open up."

"I hope you didn't break anything valuable."

"No, I stopped at Goodwill a week ago to buy things for this showdown. Everything's fine now. Good night, son. Don't stay up too late."

Lynne left the room and closed the door behind her. Violet listened to the sound of pages being turned and was on the verge of sleep when she heard the soft thump of the book being put on the nightstand. Jesse stretched out beside her and gathered her against his chest. Her body hummed with contentment as he buried his face in her hair and took a deep breath.

"Jesse?"

He stiffened. "Yeah?"

"Promise you won't leave me."

He sighed into her hair. "Vi."

She twisted her hand in his shirt. "We need to stick together."

"I don't—"

She tilted her head back, so she could see his shadowed face. "You love me, don't you?"

He stared at her, eyes unreadable in the dim light.

She thumped his chest. "Hello!"

"Yeah," he said as he ran a hand down her spine.

"Yeah, *what?*"

He sighed. "I love you."

"And I love you." She pressed as close as possible. "We need to stay together. We're a unit that nothing can tear apart. You know I have abandonment issues."

"Go to sleep, Vi," he said, voice thick with amusement.

"Don't laugh at my abandonment issues!"

"I'm not."

"You are! You're not taking me seriously!"

His thumb brushed over her lips. "Hush."

"You better not leave me to shoot guns in the military," she growled.

"Sleep," he murmured.

His fingers tunneled through her hair and massaged, easing her into sweet, dreamless slumber.

# CHAPTER 8

She woke in mid-fall. She let out a stifled shriek and flailed before she collided with something hard and unyielding.

"I got you."

She blinked up at Jesse as he toted her across a badly lit parking lot. "Wus happening?" she slurred as she tried to get her bearings.

"Got a room."

She started. "What?"

"It's midnight. We'll crash here for a couple of hours and finish the drive tomorrow."

"I can drive," she offered and tried to clear the cobwebs from her cloudy mind.

"No, you can't," he said as he shouldered through a door and dumped her on the bed. "I'm going to get our bags."

"But I can—"

He slammed the door behind him. She sat there, dizzy and exhausted, despite her catnaps. Throughout the day, she slipped in and out of consciousness. It was awful to wake every hour and realize they were still on the road. She glanced around the room, which seemed worn, but clean. As she stared dazedly at the blank TV, the door opened, and Jesse came in with his pack and her duffel. He set both on the floor before he locked the door and fell face down on the bed.

"Are you okay?" she asked belatedly.

He grunted. "Falling asleep at the wheel. Lots of animals on the road. Not worth it. Need sleep."

Resting for the night was logical, but it extended their time together. She eyed his unmoving form for a minute before she heard deep, even breathing. He was clearly exhausted, and no wonder. They left Salt Lake City around six in the morning. He had been driving for eighteen hours. She grabbed her phone and sat in a chair by the window. According to her phone, they were in Texas, about five hours from home. That wasn't too bad. She messaged her friends and parents and sent them their location, even though they were probably asleep. Tomorrow, it would be over. They would be around friends and family, and she would do her best to avoid Jesse and his psychotic episodes.

She grabbed her duffel and went into the bathroom. She showered, brushed her teeth, and smeared lotion over her dry skin. She leaned toward the mirror and examined the bite on her neck. He hadn't broken the skin, but it was red and swollen. What the fuck was wrong with him? Her ear was fine, but there was a dark smudge on her breast from his rough handling, and she was sore and achy. Her eyes were bloodshot, hair a frizzy mess, and she was trembling. It could be because she had been eating junk food all day. Or maybe it was stress and the emotional overload. Realistically, it was probably all those things combined.

It was one in the morning, which made six days since

she had come home to Austin and discovered Lynne's diagnosis and come face to face with Jesse. A week ago, her biggest worry was a job and where she would live. That seemed like a piece of cake compared to what she was dealing with now.

She stared at her reflection, eyes glassy, jaw set. On the outside, she looked unhappy, and a touch pissed. Beneath the surface, she was spiraling. If she was a different kind of person, she would have shot Jesse with one of the guns her father kept in the safe. If she was a different kind of person, she could have overcome her nightmarish teenage years and made something of herself—become a guidance counselor and helped others with their trauma and replaced the bad with good. Instead, she was this...

*You dropped out of school, can't keep a job, and bang anyone who catches your eye.*

She looked away from her reflection as her eyes stung with tears. Fuck. Against her will, her mind began to replay their encounter today in excruciating detail. Even now, she could feel the imprint of the tiles against her back and Jesse's strength as he effortlessly held her in place while he fucked her. She screwed her eyes shut and bit back a moan as her pussy spasmed. Self-loathing cascaded through her. She sank to her knees with her hands over her head. She climaxed. Every. Fucking. Time. It was no wonder he didn't stop. Her mouth said one thing while her body did another. She was fucked up. She wasn't supposed to respond to him, but she did.

When the urge to vomit had passed, she rose, using the counter to brace herself. She felt sick and had sea legs. She popped vitamins and guzzled water before she emerged from the bathroom. She paused at the foot of the king-sized bed and listened to his heavy breathing. Out like a light, just the way she liked him. Another annoying thing about Jesse—he could sleep anytime, anywhere. He dropped off easily, while she spent hours trying to shut her mind off. His lack of conscience probably helped him a lot in that department. Fucker.

There was no way in hell she was going to sleep in that bed with him. Her only choices were the chairs by the window or the discolored carpet. She could imagine how filthy the floor was. She turned both chairs towards each other so she could prop her legs up and make an awkward nest. It was extremely uncomfortable, but it was only one night. Tomorrow, she would be home. She repeated that to herself as she shifted restlessly, trying to find a position that didn't hurt.

She listened to the cars coming and going and pulled back the curtain to look outside. She spotted their massive moving truck on the far side of the parking lot with her Jeep still on the trailer. Although she would never admit it to him, she knew there was no way in hell she could have done this on her own. She resented that he barged in uninvited, but he treated her move as if it were his and footed the bill for the airline tickets, rental truck, fuel, and now a motel room. Her feelings for him were a complicated mix of begrudging gratitude, fury, resentment, and embarrassment. Her eyes moved to him. He hadn't bothered to take off his boots. She intended to drive part of the way, but between the size of the truck and trailer and that pit stop fuck, she decided to let him handle it, and he had without complaint.

Her mind swung from one thing to the next, keeping her awake when she desperately needed sleep. In between light dozes, she kept looking out the window, expecting to see the first hint of sunlight through the curtains.

She woke in mid-lift. "Wha—?"

"You're a pain in the ass," Jesse growled as he carried her to the bed.

She struck out and hit something. He cursed and dropped her on the mattress, which wasn't as soft as it looked. She lost her breath and tried to roll away, but she wasn't fully awake and ended up in the middle of the bed.

"You hit my fucking ear," he growled before he launched himself at her.

"Jesse, *no!*"

Her hands were knocked to the side as he pinned her beneath his bulk. His hairy leg slid over her smooth ones and the fog cleared enough for her to realize that he had removed almost all his clothes aside from his briefs.

"Jesse—"

"Hush," he said roughly as he pulled her more securely against him and buried his face in the pillow beside her. "I need sleep."

"I don't want to sleep with you!"

"Too bad."

She slapped his side, but that didn't get a reaction from him. She stared at the ceiling. It was still dark out. The only source of light came from the bathroom, which he must have used before he noticed she was sleeping on the chair.

"Get off me," she said.

His hand stroked down her side. "Go to sleep."

"I *was!*"

"We'll sleep better like this."

"How many times do I have to tell you, I don't want you touching me?" she hissed.

"Relax."

His words were slurred from fatigue. Clearly, he wasn't in any state to do anything sexual.

"Can you move over? Why are you on top of me?"

"Like it," he said and inhaled deep. "You smell like home."

"What?"

His even breathing told her he'd drifted off to sleep again. Even as she tried to figure a way out of this, her eyelids drooped. His weight had a drugging effect on her. Even as she fought it, her mind began to power down, convinced she was safe enough to get some rest.

---

SHE WOKE ON A MOAN. HER EYES OPENED. SHE WAS ON HER SIDE facing the window. She knew where she was, with whom, and that her body was on fire. There was an arm banded across her chest, keeping her in place as Jesse rocked in and out of her.

She had always been a sucker for this position with past lovers. Intimate, but since she was facing away, she didn't have to maintain eye contact. If the guy knew what he was doing, it was a great position to hit her G spot. Her cheek was flush to the mattress, one hand twisted in the sheets as her body moved with his. His gentle thrusts were driving her crazy. A distant part of her mind screeched, *What the hell are you doing? Run! Fight!* Instead, she lay there, boneless, wanton, swimming in sleep and sex.

"You with me?" he murmured in her hair.

She shut her eyes against the sunlight seeping through the curtains. Another day, another fuck. When he dropped her in bed last night, she knew this was how she would wake up. He never failed to take advantage. Her body felt as if it had been doused in peppermint. She was tingling all over as he kept her right on the edge. She was too far gone to put up a fight. His hand brushed over her breasts before it came to the base of her throat.

"Violet."

She clenched her teeth. Why did he have to talk? He never used to. Why didn't he just fuck her and get it over with?

"Violet."

*"What?"*

He tipped her on her back while he stayed on his side and draped her thighs over his. His hair was tousled, eyes bloodshot, and he was in desperate need of a shave. His thumb brushed over the apple of her cheek. She didn't want to see him as he fucked her. While he was behind her, she could suspend reality, but this... She turned her face away.

"Look at me."

"No."

He gripped her jaw, forcing her to face him. "I told you how I feel about that word."

She lashed out, but he was ready. He grabbed her wrist and pinned it to the mattress.

"Let me in, Vi," he growled against her sweaty temple.

"Never!"

He planted himself so deep, she grunted.

"You want me to force you so you can hate me, but deep down you know this is where you want to be."

"You're wrong!"

"Am I? Then why are you soaking wet? If you hate this, why are you squeezing me so goddamn tight?"

"Finish it," she said through clenched teeth.

"I'm not in a hurry," he said lazily as he changed his rhythm, making her body arch. "I want this to last."

"I don't."

"You don't always get what you want out of life," he chided as he kissed the side of her face. "Let me make you feel good."

His hand coasted down her body and slid between her legs. Her eyes collided with his as he rubbed her clit. He was watching every fleeting expression that crossed her face. He was analyzing and cataloguing so he would have more ammunition against her. She bared her teeth and clawed his arm, but he didn't budge.

"Stop messing with me." He made her into his plaything, and she resented it with every fiber of her being. "I'm a person, not a fuck doll."

He frowned. "I don't think of you like that."

"Then why are you doing this?"

"Because you're lying to yourself. Your mouth spits lies, but your body speaks the truth. Forget everything and just feel, Violet."

When he applied pressure to the right spot, she tossed her head back and forth. His thrusts became more forceful. Her head spun as he kissed her, applying layer after layer of sensation until she forgot to hate him.

"Tell me you want me."

His voice came from a long way off. She didn't focus on it. She was almost there... He gripped her face and gave it a sharp shake.

"Look at me," he ordered.

It took considerable effort to obey his dictate when her body was ready for take-off. When she focused on him, his grip gentled and he stroked her cheek.

"Tell me, Violet."

"What?" She sent her hand down her body to finish the job, but he captured it and twined their fingers together.

"No touching yourself. That's my job."

"You're not doing it!" she spat.

He gave her a pained grin. "Frustrated, Vi?"

"I hate you!"

He kissed the corner of her mouth. "You need to stop saying that."

"You need to stop torturing me," she panted and lifted her leg to change the way he was fucking her. "Uh, *yes.*"

"You know it isn't like this with anyone else." His breath hitched as she moved on him. He gripped her waist to stop her, but then he groaned and buried his face in her hair. "Fuck me. This is how it's supposed to be between us."

When he increased the tempo, tears leaked out of the corner of her eyes.

He glared at her with stormy eyes. "You feel that, Vi? This is bliss. There's nothing else like it on the planet. No one comes close for either of us. Admit it."

Her head thrashed as the crescendo built.

"Please," she begged.

"Please what?"

She let out an enraged bellow and threw herself at him. The only reason she got him on his back was because he wasn't expecting it. He clamped his hands on her to stop her from getting away, but that wasn't her goal. She straddled him and braced her hands on his chest. She tipped her head back and mindlessly rode him for her pleasure. She was too lost to care what she looked like with her hair loose, mouth open as she gasped and moaned. When lightning struck, she screamed. He yanked her down and covered her mouth with his. He gripped her ass to hold her in place as he began to thrust. When her orgasm hit, she pounded her fist into the mattress while he let out a loud, guttural groan and said her name.

She slumped over him in a state of satiated shock. It had never been this good.

"Okay?" he murmured.

As she shifted away, his hands smoothed down her back.

"Wait."

"We need to get going."

He kissed her neck. "We're close to home. We have time," he said in a lazy voice.

His hand sifted through her hair, reminding her of all the times he had played with it or braided it. Her eyes stung as past and present clashed. She missed this part of him. The gentle, affectionate Jesse who made her feel loved and protected. It had been so long since someone touched her like this. She didn't allow anyone close enough to coddle her. Even as she longed for her innocent past, she was aware of his dick still throbbing inside her and the smell of sex permeating the air. There was no going back.

"What's wrong?" he rumbled.

"Everything," she whispered.

She grunted as he rolled her beneath him. He braced himself over her and smoothed her tangled hair back from her face.

"Don't cry," he ordered roughly as he kissed away her tears.

She placed her hand on his chest. "We can't keep doing this."

He sat up. She moaned as he withdrew from her. He knelt between her spread thighs. She wasn't surprised when his hand slid inside her.

"I want to be a good man. In every aspect of my life, I'm

a model citizen." His eyes flicked up to hers. "Except when it comes to you."

She tried to scoot away, but he gripped her hip, warning her to stay still.

"I've broken laws, vows, and my own code to have you. I thought I had it under control, that I would see you after all this time and feel nothing." He shook his head as he looked down at his fingers sunk inside her. "But it doesn't matter how much time's passed. I had to touch, taste. I'd pay any price to possess you." He pressed his face against her belly. "I *need*, Violet."

As his fingers stroked, her toes curled.

"Mom's days are numbered and all I can think about is losing myself in you." His voice was so low, she could barely understand him. "Love me back, Vi."

An invisible pick pierced her chest and sank deep. "What?"

He lifted his head, blue eyes spearing hers. "I've been in love with you since I was fourteen."

Her body reacted before her mind could process his words. Her foot landed on his shoulder and sent him reeling back. She rolled off the bed and faced him with her hands clenched into fists.

"How dare you say that to me? You don't know the meaning of that word!"

"I know exactly what it means."

"You don't love me! If you did, you wouldn't have done all this!" She jabbed her finger at the bed. "This is sex, not love. It's lust, greedy, sinful..."

"You see it the way you want to."

She stomped her foot. "I see it the way it *is*! You took what you had no right to take! And you're *still* taking! You stole everything from me and have the nerve to say you love me?"

He shrugged. "Love can make monsters out of men when it's not returned."

Her mind went blank. There was no sound in the room aside from her ragged breathing, but inside, she was in the eye of an emotional storm. Before her mind could bolt, she held up a hand. "No."

"No?"

He was a master manipulator and pathological liar. She wasn't going to play into his hands. He was toying with her. He wasn't satisfied with owning her body, he wanted her mind too. Fuck that.

"I'm going to shower," she announced. "And then we're leaving."

She averted her face as she headed to the bathroom. She locked the door, climbed into the shower, and stared at the yellowed walls as water beat down on her head.

After everything he had done to her, he *dared* utter that word? Did he think that word absolved him of his crimes? Justified his actions? No. Love had no place in their relationship, and she'd be damned if she trusted anything that came out of his mouth.

She stepped out of the tub and wrapped a towel around her hair and then her body. She glanced at the door. She didn't want to go out there. He was making an already bad situation even worse. They had five hours left until they reached Austin, but even ten more minutes in his presence was too long. She had dreaded facing him and convinced herself that it couldn't be as bad as she imagined, but it was worse. He was determined to bring up a past she buried long ago. Her jaw ached from clenching her teeth. He thought she was stupid enough to believe he had feelings for her. She wasn't naive. He stole her innocence years ago.

She took a deep breath and put her shoulders back. Five more hours. She could do this. She had to. She got through the worst of the trip yesterday. They were so close to home. Lynne and Dad were waiting on them. She could withstand anything he wanted to throw at her, and then it would be over.

She yanked open the door with a defiant scowl, but her bravado was for nothing. He was sitting on the bed talking to Lynne on his cell phone.

"We needed some rest, so we got a room for the night," Jesse said.

His voice was lighthearted and back to its normal cadence. He was a class act.

"I'm glad you two are being so responsible and doing this trip safely," Lynne said while on speaker.

"Safe is my middle name."

Violet cast him a disgusted look as she knelt beside her duffel. He pulled on jeans, but didn't bother to button them. She couldn't resist giving his body a once over. Yes, she'd fucked him numerous times since she picked him up from the airport, but she had always been focused more on fighting than taking in his body. He was ripped. He'd always had a nice body since he was an athlete. Before he'd been broad and lean, and now he was just... huge. He had defined abs, and the veins stood out on his arms. There wasn't an ounce of fat on him. He could be Captain America's body double.

If she took a picture of him right now, it would be the perfect ad for a male gigolo. His jeans rode low on his hips, hair tousled, and the wrecked bed told its own story.

Women would pay well for one night with him. If he wore his uniform, he could make even more money. Another career path if he decided to leave the military.

"We're going to grab breakfast before we head out and be home by late afternoon," Jesse said.

His tone warm and easy. He was back to being the good son while her body still throbbed from his attention. Seriously? She wanted to hurl her shoe at his head.

"Knowing you're there with Violet makes us feel so much better. Have you two been having fun?" Lynne asked.

"Yes."

Violet ground her teeth as he told what whopping lie.

"We've been taking in the sights and talking about the past."

At that, Violet whipped her head around. Their eyes locked.

"I'm so glad we have this time together," Jesse said and winked at her.

"Fuck you," she mouthed, and he smiled.

"Here, talk to Vi. I need to take a shower and feed her. She's grumpy."

Jesse tossed the phone on her duffel before he strode to the bathroom.

"Violet?"

Lightheaded with rage, she tried to gentle her voice as she said, "Hey, Mom. How are you?"

"I'm good. I've been worried about you two but knowing you're in Texas makes me feel better. You haven't been taking many pictures."

She cleared her throat. "Yeah, no. Sorry. It's been super hectic."

"I'm sure. You two got everything wrapped up so

quickly. I'm so glad. Just a little further and then you'll be home."

"Right," she said as she got dressed.

"I'm not trying to be pushy, but what are your thoughts on heading to Florida the day after tomorrow? Is that too soon? Do you need more time to get settled or—"

"No, that sounds perfect. Let's head to the beach." She needed as much activity as possible.

"Yay! We're on the same wavelength."

Her anger was tempered by Lynne's excitement and good cheer. Just hearing Mom's voice made her feel better. Lynne was an anchor in her otherwise messed up world. All she wanted to do was curl up beside Lynne and just be. It was fucked up that she was seeking comfort from her mom when she should be giving it, but she felt so fucking lost and needed her more than ever.

"I can't wait to get home," she said.

"Me either. Having both of my babies' here..." Lynne's voice hitched suspiciously.

She walked to the window as she heard the shower cut off in the bathroom.

"Don't, Mom," she begged.

"I know, I'm sorry. I'm just so happy. You two are my world."

She swallowed hard. "And you're mine."

"Well, you'll be here soon enough. Take pictures, have fun, and be safe."

"I love you."

"I love you more," Lynne said with a sniffle. "I'll see you soon."

As she hung up, she saw that Jesse had over fifty unread text messages. She, in comparison, had no messages aside from the group texts with her parents and Reese and Meg. Hopefully, after she moved home, she would get reacquainted with classmates and beef up her social life. No more living in the past, no more isolating herself because of Jesse. No. She was going to live, and that started now.

# CHAPTER 9

Jesse came out of the bathroom as she repacked her duffel. "There's a diner next door."

"I'm not hungry."

"You're eating."

She swung around to yell at him and immediately turned away. He was buck naked. The view from the back was just as good as the front. Contoured thighs, ass, back. She had never been one to goggle at men's bodies, but his was phenomenal. There was a saying, "Never trust a pretty face." Usually, it was applied to women, but in her case, her stepbrother was the epitome of pretty outside, ugly insides.

She was miffed that by the time she had zipped her bag, he was dressed and ready to go with his pack on his shoulder. He held the door open for her. As she passed, she averted her face, before she marched across the mostly empty parking lot. It was a sunny day without a cloud in the sky. When she tried to climb in the cab, he grabbed the waistband of her pants and yanked her back out.

"Eat," he said.

She smacked his hand. "I told you—"

She ground her teeth as he tossed her duffel and his pack in and locked the truck.

"We don't have time for this," she snapped.

"We do, and I'm hungry," he said as he pushed her toward the diner.

She had no choice but to go with him.

The diner was hopping. The moment she stepped through the door, the smell of bacon and maple syrup made her stomach rumble. She and Jesse waited while a frazzled waitress searched for an open table.

"We can sit at the counter," Jesse offered.

"All right. Make yourselves at home," the waitress said.

Jesse's hand landed on Violet's lower back. She quickly stepped away and gave him a withering look before she navigated through the cramped, packed diner. The counter was occupied mostly by trucker's and old men chatting over their morning coffee. They found a spot between two sets of men, who did double takes when she took a seat. She grabbed the menu and perused it before she glanced at the old man beside her, who was staring openly.

"Morning," she said.

"It's turning out to be a good one," he said with a wink.

She relaxed and tapped the menu. "What's good?"

"Depends on what you got a hankering for," he drawled.

"I want something sweet and salty."

He grinned. "You're my kind of gal. You should get French toast with some meat on the side."

"That sounds great."

When she opened the menu, he pointed out her options.

"Thanks," she said as the waitress stepped up.

"What'll you have?"

When she gave her order, the old man gave her a thumbs up before he turned back to his friend, who was reading a newspaper and munching on toast.

"You military?"

She glanced to the right to see the burly trucker beside Jesse looking him up and down.

"Yeah. Air Force," Jesse said.

The man tipped his hat. "Thank you for your service."

She was surprised, pleased, and then annoyed when they launched into military talk. Jesse couldn't go anywhere without being acknowledged, honored, and admired. The surrounding men were all listening and nodding as he explained where he had been stationed and his last two years in remote Alaska. She didn't want to listen, but it was impossible not to when he was sitting right beside her. She was intrigued despite herself as he told stories about the men in his unit, the friends he'd lost, and that he was heading to Japan next.

"Is this your lady?" one of the truckers asked.

She whipped her head around, mouth full of French toast. Jesse's eyes crinkled at the corners when he saw her dilemma.

"Yeah," he said as he rubbed her back. "This is Violet."

"You got a good man here, miss. Not many guys still have old-fashioned values nowadays. You better hang onto him."

The trucker shook Jesse's hand and left with his buddies.

She swallowed and glared at Jesse as he ate his omelet. "Really?"

He stabbed a piece of French toast and ate it before she could stop him. "These are good."

"You're such an ass," she hissed.

He examined her for a moment. "You didn't get your coffee. That's why you're cranky."

Her mouth sagged. He used the L word, fucked her *again*, told strangers she was his, and didn't think she had grounds to be upset? "You're a goddamn psycho."

He glanced at his watch. "Finish your food. I want to be on the road within the hour."

She hopped off her stool and held out her hand. "Give me the keys. I'll wait in the truck."

"It's hot," he said.

"I don't care!"

He dropped the keys in her hand. She stalked out of the diner and realized halfway across the parking lot that he had picked up another tab for her. Oh, well. She climbed into the cab, rolled down the windows, and waited. He was right. It was hot, uncomfortably so. If she didn't give a damn, she would have run the air conditioner, but she didn't want to waste fuel. Apparently, she still had a conscience, unlike him.

She texted her friends to let them know she would be in Austin in a few hours and watched the morning traffic ebb and flow. She was sweating and starting to wonder if he was making her wait on purpose when she saw him striding toward her. Relieved, she started up the truck and leaned toward the vents to cool down.

"Here."

She glanced at him and blinked when she saw that he was holding an iced coffee. She took the cup and gave it a wary sniff.

"What?"

"You wouldn't put anything in this, would you?"

He buckled his seat belt. "What would I need to drug you for?"

Right. He got everything he wanted from her.

He pulled out of the parking lot and navigated through the small town before he found his way onto the interstate. She took a tentative sip and let her eyes flutter shut. It was an excellent white mocha. She bit back a moan.

"Good?"

She opened her eyes and saw he was watching her.

"Yes," she said grudgingly, and then waved a hand. "Eyes on the road!"

He grinned as he obeyed her order. She sat back and despite what occurred in the motel room, her spirits began to lift. She was almost home. Soon, they would be with Lynne and her father and Jesse would be heading off to Japan. She would settle in Texas and set about recovering financially, emotionally, mentally. Then, she would figure out what to do with her life.

One good thing came out of facing Jesse again. He wasn't the bogeyman under her bed any longer. He was a psycho, but one she could handle. She faced him and lived to tell the tale. For now, she would play nice for their parent's sake. Neither of them would rock the boat on that front, but in the future, she would go back to avoiding him at all costs.

Would Jesse come back to Texas if Lynne was no longer around? A surge of ambivalent emotions swept through her. Lynne was the only family he had. After she was gone, he would have no one. Well, he would have Dad. She glanced at Jesse out of the corner of her eye. Today, he added a trucker's hat to his ensemble, but everything else was the same. He hadn't shaved, which gave him a five o'clock shadow. On the surface he seemed content, but the tales he shared in the diner told a different story. He had lost many friends and people he respected since he had joined the military, and although he had glossed over the details, she could read between the lines. His five years in the military thus far hadn't been a picnic.

She wrestled with herself. She didn't want to engage him in conversation or show empathy because he would get the wrong idea, but... "I'm sorry about your friend."

Out of the corner of her eye, she saw his head turn in her direction.

"What?"

She waved her hand. "You were talking about him in the diner. Eric."

He nodded. "Yeah."

When he said nothing more, she added, "Jeremy too."

"That was a tough one."

She pursed her lips. "Is... is your job dangerous?"

He shrugged. "There's always risk."

"A *lot* of risk?"

"Worried about me, Vi? I thought you hated me."

She bristled. "I do."

"Then what's with the sudden concern?"

"Dad would be upset," she quipped. "Why have so many of your friends passed?"

"Shit happens."

"How can you sound so casual about death?"

"Death's been a constant presence in my life from when I was very young. When I was six, both of my grandfather's died within weeks of each other and my grandmothers went a couple of years later. Then there was my dad." He shook his head. "Death's inevitable."

"So, you're *okay* with Lynne going?"

He frowned. "Of course not. Just because you know it's coming doesn't make it any easier."

"Then, how—?"

"I know there's nothing I can do, so I accept it, and focus on spending as much time as possible with her."

"We're heading to Florida the day after tomorrow."

"Good."

She stared out the window. The mountains and desert had given way to flat lands as far as the eye could see. They passed fields of crops, oil rigs, and green pastures. The atmosphere in the cab wasn't as hostile as it had been yesterday. It should be worse today, especially after what transpired in the motel room, but she chose to blank it from her mind.

It was easier to act like it never happened than to ponder his motives. That pastime would drive her insane. She thought she knew Jesse better than anyone else until he started acting out of character.

It bothered her that despite everything he had put her through, there was an easiness between them that carried over from their childhood. Their familial bond hadn't been severed despite their tumultuous relationship. They knew each other's preferences and habits and may have spent half a decade apart, but their core was still the same, which gave them common ground. When they were kids, she thought they could read each other's minds. That was before he ruined their relationship with sex.

*I want to be a good man.*

He could be. He just had to stop his horny, manic episodes. When he was with her, he was a completely different person. With everyone else, he was courteous, patient, helpful. That's the boy she had grown up with, the one she loved. She would do anything for him... and had for a while, even though she knew it was wrong. Maybe that's what she hated most. Her desire to please him trumped rational thought, her self-respect, and propriety. She let it go on too long before she came to her senses and started fighting back.

Her mood began to dip. She tried to ignore the heaviness in her chest and the dark wave that swept over her, obliterating the burst of optimism she got while drinking her white mocha. Her moods were like the tides—high, low. Sometimes tsunamis swept in, and she didn't come up for air for days. That feeling of excitement and homecoming turned to ash as her spirit sank like a stone.

As if he sensed the change, Jesse said her name.

"Don't," she sighed.

"Don't what?"

She shook her head. "I just want to get through this in one piece."

"Get through what?"

Lynne's death and whatever else occurred before his departure.

Silence enfolded the cab. She leaned her head against the window and stared at the landscape, but she wasn't taking it in. Memories floated to the surface—good, bad, and ugly.

"When my dad died, I thought my life was over," Jesse said.

She tensed.

"He was my world, my hero. Mom did her best to fill the gap, but it wasn't the same. She dated a couple of guys. None of them lasted long."

They passed a grove of trees with a river running through it before they came upon open, untouched land with a lone farmhouse in the distance.

"Isaac didn't cater to me or try to make me like him. I didn't know how to take that. He was a firefighter, which was cool, but not as cool as my dad being in the military.

When Mom mentioned he had a daughter, I told her that wouldn't do. I didn't want anything to do with a prissy girl. And then we met at the park. You weren't what I expected."

She remembered that day. Dad had never introduced her to a girlfriend before. She'd been ecstatic. She had been trying to set Dad up with one of the ladies from church for years. She was tired of being shuffled from family to family when he had to work. When she met Lynne, she instinctively knew she was perfect for her father.

"You were dressed like a boy in a striped, green shirt and khaki shorts," Jesse continued. "Your hair was messy and tangled and when we played soccer, you kicked me in the shin to get the ball. You were aggressive, competitive—the complete opposite to every girl I knew. You got in my face and challenged me. You called me names and taunted me when I refused to play as rough as you."

The images he evoked caused a strange flurry in her chest. "I don't want to talk about this."

"You welcomed us in, wanted us around all the time, and cried when we left. You clung to me, made me feel needed, and looked up to me."

Her stomach lurched. "Stop."

"I fell in love with you the day we met and never snapped out of it."

She rolled the window down to drown out his voice.

"Every year it got worse until I couldn't take it anymore—"

"Pull over!"

"You didn't see—Fuck, Violet, *don't!*"

Even as she shoved her door open, she felt a hand twist in her shirt, hauling her backward. The truck swerved and Jesse cursed.

"Pull the fuck over!" she bellowed.

He pulled off the state highway beside a field of flowers. She hopped out of the truck and marched through the high grass, uncaring about the stains she was getting on her jeans or the fact that she could step on snakes and God knew what else. She didn't care. She stopped and braced her hands on her knees as she tried to catch her breath.

"Vi."

He was right behind her. Of course, he was. He couldn't give her a fucking moment.

"You need to back off," she warned.

"I gave you five years."

She whirled around to face him. "You didn't *give* me five years. You went into the Air Force, and I made you promise to stay away!"

"And I did, until now."

He was breathing hard, chest pumping beneath his gray shirt as he faced off with her.

"The only reason I went into the Air Force is because I realized how out of control I was and the effect it was having on you. I hoped after all this time, I'd be able to restrain myself, but you make me go haywire."

"You don't *want* to help yourself! You get off on dominating me, *forcing* me—"

"I don't want to dominate you. I want *you*. Any way I can have you, I'll take you."

"You're sick."

"Maybe."

"There's no maybe about it. Anyone who's done what you have should be locked up."

He pulled off his shades so he could pierce her with eyes that reflected the unreal blue sky. The bill of his cap cast a shadow over his face, but that didn't take away from the intensity of his stare.

"You could have made that happen. Why didn't you?"

When she tried to walk away, he blocked her path.

"No, answer me. If you wanted me to stop, if you hated me so much, why didn't you tell someone?"

"Who would believe me? Even *I* couldn't believe what was happening and you were doing it to *me*! Who would believe perfect Jesse Sampson was fucking his sister? You're the best actor I've ever met. You're able to turn it on and off like *that*." She snapped her fingers in his face. "You did me dirty and then carried on with your day as if nothing happened. You *still* do that!" She rubbed the place where her punctured heart thudded. "And Mom and Dad would die if they knew. You know that."

A warm breeze tugged her hair as the sun beamed down on them. Volatile emotions tumbled around inside her. She dimly noted that she had traveled further from the truck than she intended. Jesse stood between her and freedom, a silent declaration that she wasn't going anywhere until he allowed it.

"What do you want from me?" she demanded.

"I want you."

"You've had me!"

His hand slashed through the air. "Your body isn't enough. I want *you*."

"That's never going to happen."

Her heart slammed against her ribs as he invaded her space, making her feel trapped even though they stood in an empty field with miles of open land around them.

"I fell for you before Mom taught you how to dress or what it meant to be a woman. You bloomed right in front of me and started attracting and picking the worst guys to date. You made my life a fucking hell."

"And that's my fault? How was I supposed to know?"

There was a minute shift in his expression that made her stomach clench.

"You knew how I felt about you," he growled. "You woke up that night, you looked right at me."

Her heart careened into her throat. She backed away. "We aren't doing this!"

He grabbed her shoulders, halting her escape.

"We are," he gritted.

"You're fucked up!" She beat her fists against his chest. "You were sneaking into my room at night and jerking off on me! Why—what—who *does* that?"

"A desperate, horny teenager," he said in a flat, unapologetic tone. "I was obsessed. I stole your underwear at first, but that wasn't enough."

Her mouth watered as panic spread through her. She looked around, even though she knew they were alone. This was their fucked-up history, the beginning of the deterioration of their relationship. These were things she had wiped from her memory, that were so taboo she vowed never to tell a soul, and here he was, laying it out in broad daylight.

"You were turned on by it, Vi. I saw your hand moving beneath the covers. You were touching yourself while I—"

"Stop!" she screamed and ripped out of his hold so she could pace, hands swiping at the cold sweat that covered her skin.

"You're so deep in denial, I don't know how to reach you," he said as he dogged her steps. "You want to act like none of this happened, but it did and it's still happening. You want me, but you put on this act because you're afraid of what others will say."

She swung around to face him head on. "I don't want you!"

He didn't stop until their chests touched. He wasn't

Jesse, but he wasn't the monster either. He was someone else, a stripped-down version of himself she had never met before. His eyes glittered with wrath that didn't bode well for her. She mentally braced as his hand gripped her throat.

"You're lying to me, but what's worse is you're lying to yourself. You're so locked in your head that you don't know what's real and what isn't."

"You're my brother," she said through clenched teeth.

"Legally, not biologically, and I never saw you as a sister. I did everything in my power to let you know I saw you as more. Some part of you knew it, too."

She clawed at his hand. "Let me go!"

His hand flexed on her and she stilled. His eyes bored into hers as he leaned down, so his lips were a hair's breadth away from hers.

"You love me and not as a brother either. I could feel your eyes on me during games, in school, at church. You wanted to be with me all the time. We were so in sync with each other, we didn't even have to talk. I thought we had an understanding until you started dating."

Something dangerous flared in his eyes. His eyes moved over her face as his finger stroked her hammering pulse.

"Not only did you date other men in front of me. You picked losers. The only thing that kept me sane was believing you weren't going too far with them." His tone roughened. "And then I caught Tucker touching you and lost it."

He cocked his head as the hand on her neck went to her chin and angled it so she couldn't avoid his gaze.

"I let my body do the talking, assuming you would understand all the things I couldn't say."

She jerked her chin out of his grasp. "I can't do this."

"You have to. There's nowhere for you to run and no one to interfere. Talk to me, Vi."

"I have nothing to say to you!"

He gave her a small shake. "We can't move on if we don't settle our shit."

"I don't care if we move on. You ruined everything for sex!"

"I told you, it's not just sex."

"Love?" she spat as she tried to get away from him and failed. "I don't believe you. Love is *patient*, love is *kind*—"

"Love is cruel," he snarled. "Love is selfish. Love makes good people do terrible things. People think love is this soft, fluffy emotion that magically makes everything better. It isn't. It can fuck you up so bad, you'll never be the same."

"You can't use that word to justify what you've done!"

"It's all I have."

She shook her head. "This never should have happened between us. I want it to go back to the way it used to be. I want my brother back."

He brushed loose tendrils of hair away from her face. "You can't get back what you never had. I was your friend before I became your lover."

"You mean enemy."

"I never wanted to be your enemy. I meant to be your champion, your man, *yours*. You let me touch you, let me teach and pleasure you. It was only after that you started fighting—"

She shoved away from him. "I gave into you because I didn't know what to do. You were my first. You were showing me what it meant to be a woman, and it was *you*! I loved you and... I didn't know what I was doing, Jesse! You can't use that against me."

"I can. It's been between us from the moment we met

and once I had you under me, you gave into it for a while before we almost got caught and you panicked. Since then, you've refused to give an inch because everyone sees us as siblings. We're not, Violet."

"Mom and Dad see us that way! They'd have a heart attack!"

"If we stand together, eventually they'll have to accept—"

She stomped her foot. "What the hell are you talking about? *We're* nothing!"

He flushed with rage. "Because you won't let us be! We belong together."

She gaped at him. He was a madman. "You think you can say you love me, and it makes everything better? You have no idea what you did to me. I haven't been the same since you. I can't focus, can't breathe, can't *dream* anymore. I loved you more than I loved myself. You were my hero, my life. I idolized you. I would have done anything for you and you... You destroyed me."

"Vi."

"No!" She held up her hands as her eyes filled with hot tears. "You made me feel dirty, used, alone. You never addressed what was happening between us, and you stopped talking to me. All you wanted was sex. You made me feel like a thing rather than a person. You made me your dirty secret. That doesn't sound like love to me—" A sob interrupted her tirade.

Tears blinded her to the fact that he had moved in. When his fingers brushed over her face, she jerked back, but he wrapped her against him.

"Let me go, you son of a—"

"I'm sorry."

She stopped breathing. He cradled the back of her head and rocked her from side to side as she began to shake.

"I never meant to hurt you," he said against her temple. "I never meant to make you feel used or alone. I meant to worship you."

His hand smoothed over her quivering back as she sobbed against his chest.

"I'm sorry I didn't take more care with you. I'm sorry I didn't have enough patience. What I feel for you isn't gentle or sweet. It's this dark, insatiable craving and even after years of training and discipline in the military, I still don't know how to handle it. I'm sorry I'm not stronger."

"You can stop," she said raggedly.

His hand fisted in her hair. "You know I can't."

She punched his shoulder. "What's the point of apologizing if you aren't going to change?"

"I can't be around you and not have you."

"You can!"

"Every time I take you, it gets worse. I should stop. I should let you go. I should feel like a piece of shit for pushing you, but I need you."

As close as they were, she could see the conflicting emotions in his eyes—lust clashed with pity. She could feel him vibrating against her and didn't move for fear of pushing him over the edge. He was capable of anything.

"What we have, I've never felt with anyone else. Tell me you've felt like this with one of those assholes you used. I dare you."

Tears slid down her face. "You hurt me."

He kissed the tears away. "I know. I'm sorry. I can make it up to you. I'll give you anything you want, Vi."

She strained to get away from him. "We're both here for Mom. We should focus on her."

He clasped her face between trembling hands. "Tell me you love me."

She closed her eyes against the sight of him. "We need to go."

"I won't believe you if you say you don't."

Her hands fluttered between them. "I can't do this."

"Say it!"

"I... I did love you, but—"

He gave her a sharp shake. "No buts. You love me."

She shoved at him, but he didn't budge. "I'm not doing this with you."

"Give me something," he said harshly.

She stared at him through a haze of wet. "I already have."

"I need more."

"I don't have anything else to give you."

She jerked out of his hold and marched back to the truck. Her chest was so tight, she couldn't take a full breath. She wasn't sure if he was going to follow, but she had to get away. She would hitchhike if she had to. His words made her feel as if she had razor-thin cuts all over her body. She couldn't take another verbal blow. She was barely holding herself together.

She swiped at her eyes as she stomped through the grass and climbed back into her seat. She glanced at the GPS. Two more hours. They were so fucking close to home. She had just belted herself in when his door opened. She kept her face turned toward the window but felt his searing gaze move over her. She held her breath as silence filled the cab. Her hand went to the door handle, but she relaxed when he fired up the engine. When he pulled onto the highway, she slumped in her seat and closed her eyes.

She wasn't sure what he hoped to accomplish with this

confrontation, but they were still at an impasse. They hadn't reached any agreements or compromises. Neither of them would budge. She didn't know what to think of his declarations. He claimed he loved her, but she refused to believe him. Going down that road would only lead to more pain and heartache. She wanted a clean, happy life away from him and his lies and sexual barrages.

"I told myself this time around, I'd try to give you the words, even if you didn't accept them," he said.

She wanted to clamp her hands on her ears and sing at the top of her lungs, but that wouldn't stop him. Nothing would.

"I'm sorry, Violet."

Her eyes slid shut on a fresh flood of tears. She received the apology she had always longed for, but it was an empty one since he wasn't going to stop. Where did that leave them?

"I'm sorry that I loved you too much."

***

THE MOMENT JESSE PULLED UP TO THE HOUSE, SHE HOPPED OUT and raced up the driveway. The last two hours felt like an eternity. She had to sit there in a silent, emotional hell. She felt as if he released a hornet's nest inside of her. Thousands of angry insects ricocheted inside of her, demanding to be set free. She needed a distraction, people, anything that would drown out the words she refused to ponder.

She burst through the front door and saw Dad coming toward her. She gave him a quick hug. "Hey."

He patted her on the head. "You made it."

"Yes." She looked up. "Where's Mom?"

"Out back."

She gave him another squeeze before she headed toward the back door while he went out front to help Jesse. She found Mom sitting on the porch swing. Despite the warm day, Lynne was dressed in a jacket and long pants. She started when the door banged shut.

"Sorry. I didn't mean to startle you," Violet said as she walked forward and kissed Mom's cheek.

"You're here! Everything went okay?"

"Yes." Violet dropped onto the seat beside her. "How are you feeling?"

Lynne gave her a wan smile. "Tired, but happy. Where's Jesse?"

"He's taking care of the truck. Dad's with him."

She felt raw, confused, and in desperate need of a safe place. She rested her cheek on Lynne's bony shoulder. The comforting smell of lavender and vanilla soothed her as nothing else could.

"You and Jesse patched things up?" Lynne asked.

She tensed but covered up the telling motion by pushing off the ground to make the swing sway. "Yeah."

Lynne draped an arm around her and patted her side. "I'm glad. It hurt me to see you two drift apart. You were so close, closer than most blood siblings."

She said nothing.

Lynne sighed and rested her cheek on Violet's head. "We're family. We fight, but we should never let so much time pass without settling our differences. Life is too short for that."

Violet grunted.

"I know you don't need the lecture, but I feel the need to impart as much wisdom as I can," Lynne said in a tone filled with wry humor. "You're going to carry a heavy load when I'm gone."

Violet straightened and surveyed her. Lynne had dark circles under her eyes and, in just the few days they had been gone, seemed to have lost more weight. Seeing this strong, larger than life woman morph into a frail caricature of herself made her lightheaded with rage. Life was so unfair.

"What are you talking about?" Violet asked.

"I'm worried about them—Jesse and your father. Women are the glue that hold families together." Lynne cupped her cheek. "I need you to promise me you'll keep the family intact."

Her heart leapt into her throat. "I don't—"

"You and Isaac are all Jesse has. He's strong. He always has been, but don't let that fool you into thinking he doesn't need anyone. He's changed since he went into the military. I knew he would. Promise me you'll look out for him."

She escaped from one emotional skirmish only to run headlong into another.

"Your father is so angry. I don't know how he's going to be after I'm gone. I've been talking to Pastor Sonny about it. We're glad you're coming home, so your dad will have company."

She shut her eyes against the flood of tears.

"I'm sorry, Violet. You've had the shortest amount of time to digest this and will have the biggest responsibility after I'm gone. They need you." Lynne held her tight as a tear coursed down her cheek. "I know you can do this."

Violet swallowed hard. "I need a moment."

"We have that."

A slight breeze ruffled the leaves of the forty-foot Texas Ash trees that lined the backyard. Beyond the trees were rolling hills that went on forever. It was a tranquil, peaceful scene, but that had no effect on Violet's inner turmoil.

"I thought I had so much time," Lynne mused. "Before I found out I was sick, I was worried about paying off the mortgage and buying a new car. Now, I'm grateful for soft socks, beautiful days like this, and everyone around me."

Violet's heart tore.

"A lot of my students have stopped by. I love listening to their stories and hearing how far they've come." Lynne let out a heavy sigh. "I wish I could see where you and Jesse will end up."

"Mom."

Lynne gave her a watery smile. "You two are so young." She stoked her cheek. "Promise me you won't take anything for granted and you'll live life to the fullest. No regrets."

"I will," she promised.

Lynne's eyes tracked over her face and brushed back her tangled hair. "I couldn't ask for a better daughter."

"And I couldn't ask for a better mom," she whispered.

"I'm so glad you're here. Help me inside, honey. I want to stretch out on the couch."

Violet immediately got to her feet and put her arm around Mom's slim waist as she led her to the living room. She was taken aback by how weak Lynne was.

"Are you okay?" she asked as Lynne grabbed a blanket and huddled in on herself.

"Of course, dear. Are you excited to head to the beach?"

"Yes. I can't wait."

"We're going to have so much fun! Now, tell me all about your road trip."

She did her best to weave an interesting story but was saved by a group of Lynne's friends who stopped by for a visit. A glance out the window showed that there was a small crowd gathered around the moving truck and trailer. Dad and Jesse were talking to the neighbors, who wanted the latest scoop on their lives. Violet sighed. She would have to get used to being part of a small community again.

She busied herself by starting dinner and noted Lynne's smile of approval. When the guys finally came in, she had a pot of chili and coleslaw ready. They sat at the dining table like they had so many times in the past. She made a concentrated effort to keep a smile on her face and the mood light as she told her parents about her friends in Utah. Jesse stepped in when her energy flagged and went into great detail about the road trip. Mom took one bite of food and pushed her plate away. Violet was alarmed, but tried not to let it show. When Dad assisted Mom to their bedroom, she started to clean the kitchen. She was so tired, she felt faint.

"I got it," Jesse said.

"It's okay," she said without turning around.

When he gripped her hip, she stiffened.

"You're dead on your feet. Get some rest," he said firmly.

She wasn't going to argue with him. She walked away without a backward glance. Taking a shower was almost beyond her, but she did so, turning Mom's words over in her mind as she washed her hair and scrubbed the grime from her body.

She fell face-first into bed, hair wet, with no underwear beneath her nightgown. She was beyond caring about anything. She needed sleep before she took on tomorrow.

# CHAPTER 10

A WARM, COMFORTING WEIGHT STROKED HER STOMACH WHILE someone nuzzled her cheek. "Wake up, baby."

She moaned as she tried to come up from the murky depths.

"I made breakfast."

She could smell something tantalizing that awakened her taste buds. That was a good reason to get up, right? She struggled to get a hold of her faculties.

"We're going to unpack the truck and then return it."

Her brows came together. Truck? Unpack?

"Come on, Vi. Wake up."

Hard lips covered hers and a tongue sank into her mouth. The taste of coffee and sausage hit her a second before she remembered where she was. Her eyes opened as she shoved at the shoulder of the man crouched over her.

"What the hell are you *doing*?" she hissed and prepared to roll away when she realized her nightgown was hiked up to her waist. "What the fuck, Jesse?"

He stole another kiss before he tugged her nightgown down. "Tempting, baby, but we have work to do."

She sat up and glared at him. "What the hell are you doing in my room?"

"Would you rather Dad came to wake you and found you like this?"

She flushed. "Get out!"

"Get dressed. We have to unpack your things and return the truck. Some guys are coming over to help, and you need to decide where you want everything. Dad cleared a section of the garage if you want to put stuff in there until we come back from Florida."

With that, he walked through the bathroom to his bedroom. Hell. She rolled out of bed and heard the chatter of multiple voices coming from the dining room. She had overslept. How the hell was Jesse up? He should be in worse shape than her.

She brushed her teeth and glared at her reflection. If she had to choose between her father and Jesse finding her like that, she'd have to choose Jesse. If she hadn't been so tired, she never would have gone to bed like that. Now that she was living at home, she'd have to make sure she was always presentable, so she wouldn't give her poor father a heart attack. Her father was a man's man. It pained him to see her in anything too feminine or revealing.

When she came into the dining room, she found everyone gathered at the table. The sight of Lynne laughing with her father warmed her heart. She felt Jesse's eyes on her, but she ignored him as she made herself a plate of food and listened to their flight arrangements for tomorrow morning. She was just finishing her breakfast when some cars pulled up. She shoveled the last of the food into her mouth as Dad and Jesse went outside while a bunch of Lynne's friends swept through the door. She said her hellos and made hurried small talk before she walked out the front door.

The group of assembled men gave her pause. Brody and several other classmates had come to help, along with her father's friends—retired firefighters, police officers, and paramedics that she considered uncles. One of them caught sight of her and put a hand to his chest and staggered back.

"That can't be my baby girl," he shouted.

She laughed and ran toward him. He caught her up in his arms as if she were still a girl instead of a grown woman. She laughed as he spun her around and then gave her a bone cracking hug. She was passed from man to man and kissed bearded cheeks and even got some head noogies from the more reserved men.

They talked for an hour before they began to unload the moving truck. Thanks to Reese's organizational skills, she knew exactly what she wanted in her bedroom and what could be left in the garage to be sorted later. With so much help, it took less than an hour. Jesse and a friend returned the truck and trailer while she chatted with her uncle's and eventually broke off from the others with Brody, who had stayed by her side.

"How have you been holding up?" he asked as they settled on the rock wall under a tree.

"Okay," she said in a subdued tone.

He nodded. "Your life's been turned upside down. It's a big deal, you moving home."

"I wasn't doing that great in Utah, so it wasn't a big deal to make the leap."

"Still. You had a life there, and it's not easy to pick up and go."

She touched his arm. "I'm sorry about your dad."

He looked away. "Yeah."

Her heart turned over. His pain was a preview of what she would soon be experiencing. "You're taking care of your siblings and your mom. That's a heavy load, Brody."

He shrugged. "That's what you're supposed to do."

"Not everybody thinks that way."

He looked back at her. Her heart skipped as his eyes moved over her face in a way that wasn't merely friendly.

"I'm glad you're back, Violet."

It was her turn to look away. Her dad leaned against one of the trucks, smiling and talking to his friends about the good old days. Same stories, but they never tired of rehashing them. "Me too. I haven't seen these people in years."

"Tragedies have a way of bringing people together."

She wasn't prepared for Brody to cup her chin and turn her face back to his. This was a bold move, considering her father was within hollering distance and there were a bunch of people around. Her eyes bugged as she stared at him.

He grinned. "Why do you look so shocked?"

"You..." Out of the corner of her eye, she saw her father looking in their direction. "My dad..."

"He likes me."

She jerked out of his hold. "I don't know if he likes you *that* much," she lied. Dad had already given his blessing where Brody was concerned, but she wasn't about to tell him that.

"He isn't going in the house for his guns. I think I'm safe."

"I wouldn't chance it," she said with mock severity.

His eyes held hers. "You're worth the risk."

"Brody..."

He held up a hand. "I'm not asking for anything. I'm just letting you know I'm available."

"Available?" she echoed warily.

He jerked his head at the house. "I know you're here to support your family, but if you need someone to talk to, I'm here."

She relaxed a little. "Thanks," she said, touched by his offer.

"I wanted to state my intentions this time around."

"Intentions?"

A grin tugged at his lips. "I like you. I always have."

"As a friend."

"As more, but you didn't see me that way. Now you do."

"Says who?" she demanded.

He gave her a cocky smile. "Let's just say I can tell the difference. We did everything we could to get your attention, but you made it clear you weren't interested." He shook his head. "You have bad taste in men, honey. You chose the worst guys when you could have had your pick of the best."

She threw up her hands. "Why do people keep *saying* that?"

"Because it's true. You dated the bad boys, the loners, the freaks. You put Jesse through hell. It's no wonder he beat the crap out of Tucker after those rumors went around."

"What rumors?"

Brody's brows shot up. "You don't know?"

"No! What rumors?"

He grimaced and rubbed the back of his neck. "I thought you knew. I don't know if it's my place to—"

"Brody!"

"Tucker said he popped your cherry, and he was sharing you with his bandmates."

She shot to her feet. "He said *what*?"

Brody held up a placating hand as he rose. "It was a long time ago."

"I don't care how long ago it was! I can't believe he said that!"

"The day that rumor started circulating was the day Jesse beat the hell out of Tucker. How could you not know that?"

Because Jesse took her virginity after that confrontation with Tucker and everything else ceased to exist for her. She had no idea Tucker started such a filthy rumor. What the hell?

"I never even slept with him!" she burst out and immediately glanced at her dad.

Dad wasn't paying her any mind, and that was a good thing, since sex wasn't discussed so openly here in Texas. That was another thing she would have to remember now that she was home. Dad would go apoplectic if he heard her using such language.

"I'm glad to hear that," Brody said as he slid an arm over her shoulder and gave her a light squeeze. "He was an asshole."

"Does he still live here?" she growled.

He chuckled. "No. I think he moved to Los Angeles with his band. Never heard anything about him after that."

"What a jerk," she fumed, and suddenly wished she hadn't stopped Jesse from beating the crap out of him.

"I think your taste in men is about to improve."

She glanced up at him. "You think so?"

He had an extremely satisfied look on his face. "Apparently, I have your father's blessing. He just gave me the nod."

His eyes flicked to the left. She followed his line of sight to see Jesse hopping out of his friends' truck.

"Jesse on the other hand…" Brody's smile widened. "He's always been protective of you, and no wonder with the guys you choose. I'll have to show him my paycheck and health benefits before he lets me take you out."

She elbowed him. "Cut it out."

"Maybe your dad can vouch for me. I have honorable intentions."

"You're ridiculous," she said as Jesse and Anton came to a stop in front of them. "Hey, bro."

She was baiting the tiger, but with her dad in sight and Brody's arm around her, she was feeling safe and daring.

Jesse's eyes flicked from her to his friend. "What's this?"

He sounded calm, but she knew better.

"Vi and I are getting reacquainted," Brody said.

"Man, I called dibs!" Anton said.

Brody tucked her into his side and kissed her temple. "Vi and I have a connection."

She smacked his stomach and noticed distractedly that it was just as hard as Jesse's.

"She's here for our mom, not for all you hounds to move in on her," Jesse said.

"I know," Brody said. "I'm just letting her know who to call if she needs anything. You're not always going to be here."

Jesse focused on her. "You have to pack for our trip, don't you?"

She gave him a long look before she went on tiptoes and planted a kiss on Brody's jaw. "I'll call you if I need you."

"What about me?" Anton demanded. "My shoulder's free to cry on!"

She laughed as she went to him and gave him a hug. "You guys are crazy. Thanks for your help today."

"Of course," Anton said. "You're one of us."

That put a hitch in her step, but she smiled at them before she went inside. She did need to pack, and her room was a freaking disaster. The need to organize and nest was riding her hard. She wanted to do as much as she could before they left tomorrow, but she was waylaid by Mom's friends, who jumped on her the moment she walked through the door.

"It's so good to see you!"

"Did you get your college degree?"

"You're such a good girl, moving home to be with your parents during this time."

"Jesse's such a sweetheart for helping with your move!"

By the time the interrogation was over, she didn't have the energy to do anything. She plopped on the sofa beside Lynne and moaned.

"They mean well," Lynne said.

"I forgot what it's like to have people questioning you about your life." Violet spread her hands. "I don't have any plans, and I don't know what I'm doing."

"You don't need a plan. God will guide you," Lynne said.

She looked away, uncomfortable with the casual reference to God when she held such dirty secrets in her heart. How would Lynne feel about the sinful relationship she and Jesse had maintained throughout the years? Was that God's plan as well?

"I'll make dinner," she said and got up from the couch.

She was moving a piece of butter over the top of the

cornbread she had pulled out of the oven when Dad and Jesse walked in.

Dad clapped Jesse on the shoulder. "I'm proud of you, son. You're doing great things in the world."

Her stomach clenched as melted butter seeped into the top layer of the cornbread. It was clear that Mom and Dad were proud of Jesse serving in the military and his many accomplishments. They loved and adored him. If her parents knew what occurred between them, would that change their opinion of him?

Jesse looked at her from across the room. She held his gaze for a moment and heard the echo of the words he uttered in the motel room.

*Love can make monsters out of men when it's not returned.*

She shook her head and looked down as she continued to prepare dinner.

# CHAPTER 11

"Here."

She took the iced coffee Jesse handed her with a grunt and took a seat amongst her family and the other passengers waiting for the flight. It was early and once again, she hadn't gotten much sleep. There were a myriad of reasons why she couldn't settle, but for some reason, that tidbit Brody dropped about Tucker circled round and round in her mind.

How could a rumor she hadn't even known about bother her six years later? She knew Tucker had a reputation as a bad boy, but he'd been so sweet when they were dating. She also resented the fact that Jesse and Brody had commented on her bad taste in men. It was an ongoing joke with Reese and Meg, but she had never paid much attention to it until now. It wasn't like she went out of her way to find shitty guys. Apparently, they flocked to her. And she didn't always attract losers. She hooked her friends up with Abel and Travis. Apparently, she gave the good guys to other people and kept the freaks for herself.

When they started to board the plane, Mom and Dad

went first since Lynne was in a wheelchair to preserve her strength. Like they had the first time, she and Jesse waited while everyone rushed to get on, even though they had assigned seats.

"Thank you for helping me with my move," Violet said, staring straight ahead. It galled her to say it, but she owed him. She wouldn't have been able to do it without him.

"You're welcome."

She got up and dumped her cup before she came back and shouldered her oversized purse. The lines had gone down, so she and Jesse made their way over to the ticket agent. She pursed her lips before she rounded on him.

"Did Tucker really say he shared me with his band?" she asked in a rush.

His eyes narrowed. "Who told you that?"

"Brody brought it up yesterday."

"Brody talks too much," he said and ushered her forward with a hand on her lower back.

She dug her heels in. "Is it true?"

"Yeah."

She stiffened. "But, why would Tucker say that? I never even..."

Jesse's eyes moved over her flushed face. "He knew you were too good for him and that everyone was wondering why you were with him. He wanted to ruin your reputation so no one else would want you."

She huffed and handed her ticket over to be scanned before she walked down the short tunnel to the plane. Again, she had to wait and again, she felt the heat of him at her back. She whirled to face him.

"You believed that rumor?" When he hesitated, she demanded, "You thought I'd sleep with all those—?"

"Of course not," he snapped. "I didn't believe any of it until I caught you with him."

With his hands in her pants. That was the furthest she had ever gone with a boyfriend. She probably would have given Tucker her virginity if Jesse hadn't claimed it for himself. "Did you beat him up because of the rumor or because you caught us?"

"Both." He pushed her forward. "You shouldn't have been with him in the first place."

"Why didn't I hear about this?"

"Because I put a stop to it."

"How?"

His eyes seared hers. "I told the truth—that you had never slept with him."

She entered the plane and shuffled down the narrow aisle. She grinned at Mom and Dad before making her way to their row, which was toward the back. They hadn't been able to reserve seats together since they booked their tickets last minute. She'd been hoping she and Jesse were sitting apart, but no luck. She took the window seat while he took the aisle. She shoved her purse under the seat in front and buckled herself in.

"About Brody."

She had been expecting this. She mentally braced before she looked at him. "Yes?"

His eyes speared hers. "You shouldn't mess with the guys."

"*Mess* with them?"

"Don't encourage them."

"Like Brody said, you aren't always going to be around. I'm going to do whatever." She paused for emphasis, "Or *who*ever I want."

He grasped her chin. "You're mine."

She grasped his wrist and tugged. She dimly noted she couldn't wrap her fingers around the width of it. Everything about him was supersized. "I'm not."

"You've been mine since you were thirteen." His knuckles skimmed down her throat. "It started so innocently. Enjoying each other's company, building memories. We spent every waking moment together." His thumb brushed over her sprinting pulse. "I remember when it changed. We were camping at the lake with church friends, and you wanted to play chicken. Malcolm lifted you on his shoulders. Your legs were draped around his neck. He was holding your thighs, touching you..." His eyes darkened as his fingers left her pulse and slid between her cleavage before she jerked back. "He tried to get you to ride the jet ski with him."

She remembered that. "You made me ride with you instead."

His eyes glinted as the flight attendant launched into her safety speech in case of an emergency.

"I got to feel your arms around me, your breasts against my back," he said in a low, gravelly voice. "And I told Malcolm to keep his goddamn hands to himself."

"You're insane."

"Maybe."

"No, you *are*," she retorted.

She rolled her shoulders to brush off the effect his voice had on her. When he gripped her thigh, she tensed.

"Let Brody off easy. Anton, too."

She glared at him and smacked his hand, which didn't budge. "They're nice guys."

"I don't care."

"You have no claim on me."

"I told you how I feel about you," he said in a low voice

as his fingers glided up her bare thigh. "And even though you threw my feelings back in my face, that doesn't mean I'm going to let you go off with some other guy."

She clamped her thighs together when he tried to slip beneath her shorts.

"Are you crazy?" she hissed.

"Did you hear what I said?"

"I heard you. Will you stop touching me?"

"No."

She peeked over the seats in front of them to locate their parents. Her dad was reading a book while Lynne rested her head on his shoulder.

"We're here for Mom," she reminded him in a low undertone.

"I know," he said as the plane lurched into motion.

"Remember that and focus on her, not me. This trip is about making sure she has the time of her life."

"She will."

Violet made a clearing motion with her hands. "And that's it."

When he didn't reply, she glanced at him and wished she hadn't.

"I can't be your brother, but I'll try to be your friend," he said as his eyes moved over her face. "And make you want more."

"That'll never happen," she said and sucked in a breath as the plane lifted off the ground.

"We'll see."

He traced distracting patterns over her skin.

"You want to join the mile-high club?" he asked several minutes later.

"Only if that means I push you out of the plane, and you fall to your death."

His mouth twitched. "No, it means I fuck your brains out in a stall where any moment there could be turbulence, and we die before we get back to our seats."

"I'll pass."

"Next time," he said lazily.

She shoved his hand away. "Never! And keep your hands to yourself. I'm not here to entertain you."

---

She examined herself in the mirror. The fuchsia bikini Lynne bought her fit perfectly, but it was more revealing than anything she would have chosen. She was a t-shirt and jeans kind of girl and if she wore a bathing suit, it was a one piece. The bright color complimented her pale skin, but she felt very exposed even after tying a white sarong around her waist. Oh, well. Wearing it would make Lynne happy, and it fit well, even if it wasn't her style.

She walked out of the bathroom and surveyed their room, which was decorated like a beach cottage rather than a hotel room. Vintage pictures hung on the walls, while weathered-looking wood furniture graced the room. They had a connecting room with their parents. She and Jesse were sharing, of course, but she wasn't too worried. He was playing the good son, waiting on Lynne hand and foot. Even though the sight of him doting on Lynne warmed her heart, she reminded herself to be on her guard.

Despite everything that happened on the road trip, there was no trace of anger or resentment in his attitude toward her. He constantly had an arm slung over her shoulders. Neither of their parents thought anything of it. To them, everything was back to normal when it was anything but. Her attempts to avoid him were ignored. She fell asleep on the flight and woke to find she was using his shoulder as a pillow. When she glared at him, he laughed. Her grumpy mood lasted until they pulled up to the hotel, and she saw the sparkling blue water.

She walked toward the glass sliding door and pulled it open. She could hear the ocean from here. They were on the first floor, right on the beach. She was as giddy as a child. She wanted to sprint across the sand and dive into the water, but the sound of Lynne's voice kept her from racing outside. She turned to see what the holdup was and found Jesse staring at her. He had changed into red surf shorts, a t-shirt, and cap. She couldn't see his eyes since he wore sunglasses, but she knew what he was thinking.

"Don't even think about it," she warned before she sailed into their parents' room.

Lynne wore a sheer cover up with palm trees over her sunny bathing suit and a massive straw hat. When she saw Violet, she clapped her hands together.

"It looks great on you!" Lynne exclaimed.

When Dad saw her, his brows drew together, a predictable reaction to her wearing something so revealing. Inwardly, she shrugged. Lynne bought her suit, so if he had problems, he had to take it up with her.

"Are you ready?" she asked.

"Yep!" Lynne handed her beach bag to Dad and linked their arms together. "Let's go!"

People were milling around, but it wasn't crowded. They bypassed the pool and headed straight to the ocean. They found two loungers with an umbrella for shade and set their things on it.

"Isn't it just like you remember?" Lynne gushed as she held on to her hat, so the sea breeze wouldn't take it.

"It's even better," Violet said as she unwound the sarong and started toward the water.

"Hey."

Two fingers slipped beneath the string holding her top together. She glanced back at Jesse, who held up a tube of sunscreen.

"Yes, you better lather up. You don't want to get burned on the first day," Lynne said as she slathered white paste over her arms.

Violet held out her hand. Jesse's mouth curved as he squeezed sunscreen on her palm. Impatiently, she rubbed it over herself and knew she wasn't doing a good job, but her eyes were on the figures gliding through the aqua water.

"Turn around. Let me do your back."

She gave Jesse a long look before she turned. Rough hands slid over her. He didn't do anything inappropriate and when he was through, he was by her side as she headed to the water. The first step in was a shock. It was colder than she expected, but that didn't stop her. She dove into a gentle swell and screamed underwater before she came up laughing.

Jesse surfaced beside her. She splashed him before she caught sight of Mom and Dad wading in after them. She cheered and put her arms in the air and danced in pure joy.

"Doesn't it feel great?" she crowed.

Lynne's smile was as bright as her bathing suit. "This is exactly what I needed."

They bobbed in the water, talking and taking in the sights. Lynne tired quickly. When she had to make her way back to shore, Jesse helped his mother to the lounger and stayed with her while she and Dad swam and chatted about her road trip.

Too soon, the sun began to set. They went to their

rooms to change before making the short walk to the hotel restaurant, which looked like a massive tiki hut. There was live music and good food. When she ordered a cocktail with a slice of pineapple in it, she got a disapproving look from Dad, but he didn't comment. Lynne didn't eat at all, though she seemed happy and relaxed. When Violet fell into bed several hours later, head swimming, stomach full, and lips curled up in a smile, she knew she was going to make every moment of this vacation count.

# CHAPTER 12

Days passed in a busy blur. Naps in hammocks, swimming to her heart's content, bike riding through town, and quality time with her parents lifted the weight she had been carrying for years. She felt like the sea and sun were cleansing her, giving her a fresh start. The past didn't exist, just the here and now.

Jesse was the only blip on her horizon, but she didn't have time to worry about him when there was Lynne to tend to. She and Jesse had an unspoken agreement that one of them would always be with Lynne to give Dad time to rest as well. They catered to Lynne's every whim, not that she had many. Although Lynne's optimistic attitude never wavered, it was clear that every day was more taxing than the last.

On their last day in Florida, they watched the sun set. She and Dad lay in one hammock, while Lynne and Jesse lounged in another.

"You guys are awesome," Dad said, and placed his hand on Violet's wet, tangled hair. "I couldn't ask for better kids."

"I guess you raised us right."

He gave her a lopsided smile. "I guess so, but I can't take as much credit as I would like. I know I wasn't around as much as I should have been. Thank God for Lynne."

Violet glanced at the neighboring hammock. Lynne had the biggest smile on her face as she listened to Jesse. "Yes."

"I'm glad you aren't like your mom."

Violet's attention snapped back to her father. "I'm sorry?"

His skin had a pink hue from the sunset. His eyes were unfocused and lost in thought as he stared at the ocean. "Your mom was a selfish person. I thought she would change once she became a mother, but it only made things worse. All she wanted to do was party."

Violet could count on one hand the number of times Dad had talked about her mother, and none of them had been about her personality or the issues in their relationship.

"She wanted more out of life than to be a mom or housewife. She wanted to be famous. I thought she was joking, but one day I woke up, and she was gone." He let out a long sigh. "I went to church because I was lost and angry and needed help. The church helped me get on my feet and gave you a solid foundation. I know you were raised by a lot of people, maybe more than you wanted to be, but I did my best."

"You're a great dad."

He wrapped a burly arm around her head and kissed her brow. "You're a good girl. Sweeter than I deserve. I know I'm not good at talking about all this stuff, but I'm glad you moved home."

"Of course," she said and tried to keep her voice level, so she wouldn't ruin the moment.

"Sometimes I feel like God turned his back on me. Your mom left, and I had to raise you on my own. I had to ask others for help, which I hated doing, but I didn't have a choice. Then Lynne came along, and everything fell into place. I thought we'd grow old together, and now..."

"Dad," she whispered and squeezed his hand.

When he glanced at her, her heart tore when she saw his eyes were full of tears. "But I still have you, don't I?"

"Yes, you do."

He sighed. "One day at a time, right?"

"Right."

Once the sun sank beneath the horizon, they headed back to their rooms to shower before they ate. Halfway through dinner, Lynne said she didn't feel good. When they tried to wave down a server to take care of the bill, Lynne told them, "You two stay and enjoy your meal. I think I just need to lie down."

They watched Dad practically carry Lynne out of the restaurant. When Jesse looked at her, she saw the same worry and fear in his eyes. They ignored what Mom said and settled the bill and made their way back to the room, only to hear Lynne being violently ill. As she and Jesse rushed into the connecting room, Jesse hurried to the bathroom to help Dad support Lynne, who was so weak, she couldn't hold her head up. The toilet was covered in vomit so dark it was nearly black. When Dad tried to call an ambulance, Lynne threw a tantrum until he agreed not to.

Violet sat on the edge of her parent's bed and listened to the sound of Lynne sobbing as Dad bathed her. Violet dropped her face in her hands and fought tears.

"She's going to be okay," Jesse said.

She looked up at him. "You know she isn't."

His face was grave as he amended, "As good as she's going to be."

When Dad carried Lynne to bed, Violet rose to help. Lynne apologized profusely for interrupting dinner and ruining the mood.

"Don't, Mom," Violet said as she turned back the covers.

While Dad went to clean himself up, she slid into bed with Lynne and curled up against her.

"Are you having a good time, honey?" Lynne asked in a raspy voice.

She flinched. Lynne was ignoring her bouts of sickness and focusing on them instead. It was easier than facing her mortality. Lynne needed to know they were having a good time above all else.

"Of course. This place is spectacular," she said with as much enthusiasm as she could muster.

Lynne patted her arm. "Promise me you'll come back here someday."

She would promise anything to ease her pain. "I promise," she said instantly.

"Good. What should we watch?" Lynne asked as she reached for the remote.

"Anything."

Lynne turned on *The Three Stooges*. When Mom chuckled, she tried to join in, but knew she fell short. Her heart was lodged in her throat. Before Dad emerged from the bathroom, Lynne fell into a restless sleep. Violet listened to the sound of her rattling breaths and hugged Lynne's slight body to hers and willed life into her mother. Her tears soaked the covers as she prayed over Mom, reaching out to the God who had abandoned her long ago.

"Violet."

She raised her head and looked at Dad, who stood on the other side of the bed. Her lower lip trembled as she stared at his grave expression.

"I'll take her to the hospital once we get home tomorrow." He slid into bed on Lynne's other side. "Get some rest, kiddo."

She kissed Lynne's cheek before she walked into the connecting room. Jesse sat up in bed, hands behind his head as he watched some war documentary. She stared at her bed for a moment before she walked to the sliding door and opened it.

"Where are you going?" Jesse asked.

"For a walk."

"I'll come with you."

She glanced back at him. "I don't need an escort."

He was already on his feet and turning off the TV. "Let's go."

It was close to one in the morning as they walked around the pool, empty bar, and restaurant. It was quiet aside from the sound of the ocean in the distance. Once they reached the beach, she slipped off her slippers and held them in one hand as she walked to a pair of abandoned loungers, just past the circle of light cast by the resort.

A sliver of moon offered just enough light to see the waves crashing on shore. She dropped her slippers on the sand and walked along the beach. Jesse fell into step beside her. She wrapped her arms around herself and closed her eyes as a warm breeze caressed her chilled cheeks.

Lynne was dying. As pain cascaded through her, she stopped in her tracks.

"Violet?"

She shook her head as tears slid down her cheeks. She wanted to scream and rage but knew it would do no good. Lynne was suffering and there was nothing she could do. Lynne was the heart of their family. Once she was gone, it would never be the same. Lynne filled the void left by her biological mother; a void she hadn't realized existed until Lynne showed her unconditional love. Lynne would take a piece of her when she left.

Life seeped out of her every day. Lynne wasn't eating and had more sick moments than good ones. This morning, she caught a glimpse of the number of pills she was taking, and they weren't helping. There was nothing she could do to buy her mother time. All she could do was watch and shower her with as much love as possible. Grief nearly sent her to her knees.

"Hey."

Jesse gripped her arm to steady her.

She wrenched away and bellowed, "This isn't fair!"

She couldn't read his face in the dim light, but he said, "I know."

"I can't stand this," she said raggedly. "I feel like..." Like she wanted to howl at the moon and scream at the sky. Maybe God would hear her pleas and spare her mother.

"It's going to be okay," Jesse said in a flat tone that told her he didn't believe the empty platitude any more than she did.

"It's not," she said in an anguished whisper.

He was silent for a moment before he agreed, "No, it's not."

She covered her mouth to cover the sob building in her throat. "I... I can't... I don't know what..." She tugged at her hair as she turned in a circle, searching for help she knew she wouldn't find.

"Violet."

Something in her snapped. She marched toward the water until Jesse blocked her way.

"What the hell are you doing?" he demanded.

"What does it look like?" she spat as she pulled her sundress over her head and dropped it on the sand. "Get out of my way."

"If you want to swim, we can go to the pool."

"No." She wanted the taste of salt on her tongue and to fight the pull of the current. In a world where she had no control, she wanted a moment to feel free and unrestrained.

"Who knows what's in the water? This isn't smart."

"No one asked you to come with me," she retorted. A familiar recklessness was taking hold, her knee-jerk reaction to stress.

"Violet."

His voice was no longer emotionless, but she was too focused on her goal to notice.

"Get out of my way!"

"Fuck."

He lifted his shirt over his head. Before he had his pants off, she sprinted toward the black waves. She dove in and felt instant relief the moment she was engulfed in the chilly water. The underwater white noise drowned out her agony. She broke the surface in time to see Jesse wading toward her. The twinkle of resort lights seemed miles away.

"Don't go too deep," Jesse warned.

She ignored him as she swam to get her emotions out through strenuous exercise. Jesse kept pace with her as she did laps and fought the churning water. When she had exhausted herself, she stood submerged up to her neck, panting.

"Feel better?" Jesse asked.

Her eyes stung with tears. "No."

"Let's go in," he urged.

"Not yet."

She bent her knees, so she was floating, and let her toes skim the sand as the waves moved her back and forth.

"Talk," she said.

"What?"

"Talk about something. Anything. Distract me."

"I've been doing some research on Japan. It seems like it's going to be an interesting place to be stationed."

She relaxed a little. "How long will you be there?"

"At least a year."

"You... you like being in the military?"

"Yes."

"You think you'll be a lifer?"

"Probably. I like the lifestyle, the rules, travel, and brotherhood. I like being a part of something bigger than myself."

She nodded. "You know where you belong."

"What about you? What's on your agenda?"

"I have no idea." She shivered. Now that she wasn't on the move, the cold was getting to her, but she was reluctant to leave the water and go back to the hotel room. "I don't know what life's going to be like now that I'm home... or what it'll be like without Mom." Her voice cracked. "I have no idea what I'm doing."

He tugged her into his arms. She was too sad to fight him. She rested her face on his shoulder and wrapped her legs around his waist as they allowed themselves to flow with the water.

"We'll get past this."

"How?"

"Together."

She sniffled against his chest. "But you're such a dick."

He let out a short chuckle. "But I'm being so good right now."

She thumped his shoulder. "Can't time slow down just a little bit?" she whispered. "I need more time."

"I've been saying that most of my life," he said as he stroked her back.

She sniffled. "She's your mom. This must be worse for you than it is for me."

"It's the worst pain imaginable. Even though I've done this before, it doesn't get easier. I don't know what's worse—not knowing it's going to happen or watching it happen slowly."

His desolate tone made her reach out and cup his face. "I think it would be worse if you didn't have a chance to say goodbye. At least you got to see her again and have this time with her."

She could feel the weight of his stare even in the darkness.

"Are you going to be there for me after she's gone?" When she hesitated, he rested his forehead against hers. "I need you, Violet."

Her heart felt as if it was being squeezed. "Jesse, I—"

"I'm trying to give you what you want," he said hoarsely. "I can't do this without you. I won't survive it."

Something about his miserable tone struck a chord in her. Sensing he needed comfort just as much as she did, she wrapped her arms around him. "I'm here."

"And later?"

Her soul tore. "I..."

"Promise you won't cut me out of your life again."

Even as a small voice in the back of her mind told her not to give in, her mouth said, "I promise."

Past and present collided. They were renewing promises they made to each other as children, clinging to one another, making sure they would never be alone. They were much older, but still lost and scared. She brushed her cheek against his and found it damp. Intuition told her it wasn't the ocean. His tears had gone unnoticed in the dark.

"Don't, Jesse," she whispered.

An overwhelming urge to console him made her frame his face and kiss him. When he sucked in a breath, his mouth parted, giving her an opening for her tongue to delve in. The taste of some kind of citrus made her explore him thoroughly. His hand clenched in her hair as he held her to him, but she wasn't trying to get away.

She was the aggressor. She was drowning and needed something to keep her anchored in an unfair world where nothing made sense. Something real and tangible to keep her sane. When she arched against him, he groaned.

"Violet?"

There was a question in his voice, one she didn't want to answer verbally because it would break the spell they were under. Instead, she unwrapped her legs from his waist and tugged him toward the shore. He didn't waste any time hustling them out of the water. He was focused on the distant lounge chairs, but that was too far. She dropped to her knees in several inches of water, which disappeared as the wave retracted.

Some madness came over her. She tugged down his briefs and pumped her hand down his soft shaft before she took him in her mouth.

"Holy fuck, Violet."

He sounded stunned, and rightfully so. This was the first time she had ever initiated anything sexual between them, but she was desperate for what he could provide—

temporary oblivion and pleasure. This was wrong, but right now, she didn't care. In the darkness, it didn't count. There was no one to witness this coupling.

He stroked her hair as she suckled. She knew exactly what he wanted. He had taught her long ago. As she worked him, the warm breeze caressed her skin. Every wave that rolled in buried her thighs in soft, wet sand. She felt daring, defiant, and proudly brazen. Feeling him tremble from her touch made her feel powerful instead of weak and helpless.

"Fuck."

Jesse jerked away and leaned down to kiss her reverently. "I'm going to come in your mouth if you don't stop."

"I can—"

"Tell me what you need," he said in a voice rough with desire.

She positioned herself on her hands and knees, breasts smashed against the wet sand with her ass in the air. He needed no further urging. He knelt behind her, tugged her panties to the side, and sheathed himself in one brutal thrust. She braced her hands in the sand as he planted himself deep.

"Violet, I—"

"Just do it," she ordered.

He didn't argue. He fucked her hard. Her screams were drowned out by the waves and when he came, he sent her sprawling. She rested her cheek on the damp sand as he crouched over her, quivering.

"Violet," he moaned.

"Shh."

She didn't want to talk. She wanted to suspend reality for as long as possible. He gave her a few minutes before he carried her to the water to clean the sand and himself from her. He swiped up their clothes before they staggered across the beach to the lounge chair where she had dropped her slippers. She was surprised when he urged her to stretch out on the lounger and knelt between her shaking thighs. He was gentle as his tongue slid over her, tending to her swollen flesh. She stared up at the stars as she gave herself over to the moment and climaxed with her hand clenched in his hair.

He straightened and kissed her deeply, letting her taste herself on him. She gripped his neck to prolong the contact and when their lips separated, he hovered over her, searching her face.

"Better?" he asked.

She nodded.

"Let's go."

He dressed and had to help her because she didn't have the coordination to do it herself. When she stood, he picked her up in a fireman's carry. She was too tired to complain. When they entered their air-conditioned room, she tensed, but Jesse didn't tarry. He went straight to the bathroom and set her in the shower. She slumped against the wall and waited for him to leave. He didn't. Her eyes flared as he stepped in with her and slipped off his shorts and reached for her dress.

"What the hell are you doing?" she said in a muted shriek.

"The door's closed between the rooms."

"Why would they do that?" she asked, too distracted by this information to resist when he pulled off her dress.

"My guess is she's having a rough night, and they don't want to disturb us."

"Maybe I should—"

"Bathe," he said and turned on the shower, making her sputter.

He boxed her into the corner and kissed her silly. She punched him in the stomach, which made no impact on him. When he finally pulled away, she had to blink a couple of times because her head was spinning.

Not another word was said between them as he bathed her. She left the shower first and did her nighttime routine in record time before she crept into the room and spotted the closed door. Hastily, she dressed in the dark before she slipped into bed and pulled the covers up to her chin like a child.

She stared at the ceiling. She had done something stupid tonight. Monumentally idiotic. She waited for the rush of guilt and shame, but nothing happened. Instead, she closed her eyes, yawned, and fell asleep.

***

"Hey."

She looked up from where she was sitting on her bedroom floor, surrounded by open boxes. Jesse stood in the entrance leading into the bathroom. Her heart skipped a beat as she took in his grim look.

"Hey," she said and went back to pulling things out of a box.

As he strolled toward her, her skin prickled in alarm. This morning, they had time for a quick breakfast before they checked out of the hotel and headed to the airport. Thankfully, their seats were grouped together on the plane. She arranged Mom and Dad between her and Jesse. Once they arrived back in Texas, Dad forced Lynne to go to the hospital.

She accompanied them but was left in the waiting room. When Lynne was wheeled out a few hours later, announcing that all was well, Violet noticed that Dad didn't agree with her. He was clearly concerned, but he didn't contradict Lynne. Once they reached home, Violet whipped up dinner and spent her time by Lynne's side until she fell asleep.

It was the wee hours of the morning and since she couldn't sleep, she decided to unpack. She assumed no one was awake. She should have known better.

Jesse crouched beside her. "Are you avoiding me?"

She scooped a stack of clothes out of the box and plopped it on the carpet. "Of course not."

He gripped her chin. "I'm not playing this game with you," he said in a low growl.

She blinked. "I'm not playing a game."

He cocked his head. "Aren't you?"

She batted at his hand. "No!"

"Then what happened on the beach?" When she tried to look away, he tightened his hold on her. "You gave yourself to me, Violet."

"I was sad, and I needed—"

"Me," he interjected in a steely tone. "You needed me, Violet."

"I *don't* need you!"

In a move so swift, she wasn't sure how it happened, he pinned her on the carpet and gripped her throat as he loomed over her.

"I'm hanging on by a fucking thread here," he warned. "Mom's sick and you're... I don't know what you are. You say you hate me, that you want a sexless friend, and then you come onto me. You kissed me, bent over for me, let me pleasure you."

"It was just sex."

His eyes narrowed to slits. "It's more than that. When you're feeling lost and alone, you turn to those you trust." He rested his forehead on hers. "Damn it, Vi, I thought we sorted our shit."

"Sex solves nothing!" She braced both hands on his chest and pushed. "I was having a moment. It's gone now."

His hand flexed on her throat. "Liar."

"Don't call me a liar!"

"I love you, but right now, I want to strangle you. You're making me crazy."

"Don't say that word!"

"I'm going to say it until you believe it," he said against her lips. "I've hurt you, so you want to hurt me back. I can take it, and I'll take you whenever you give me an opening, but I'm not going to let you ignore what's between us."

His hand slid over her thin top and squeezed her breast.

"I'll never forget the sight of you sucking me off on the beach. It's etched in my memory." His hand moved down her body and slid between her legs. She jerked as he unerringly found her nub and began to rub, her thin pajama shorts no detriment to his ministrations.

"Jesse, don't!"

He kissed her. She was expecting him to be rough and brutish. The gentle, coaxing kiss took her by surprise. When he deepened the caress, her eyes fluttered shut. He kissed her with such absorption that her mind wiped clean. Her hips left the ground, so his finger could penetrate her folds.

"I love you," he rumbled as his eyes tracked over her face. "And you love me too."

Her heart slammed against her ribs. "I don't."

He kissed her forehead. "Stubborn."

He rose, leaving her prone and trembling on the floor.

She stared at him. "Jesse?"

He stood over her, gripping his erection through his sweats. "You know where to find me," he said before he walked through the connecting bathroom to his room.

She stared at the dark doorway, mind and body clashing as she struggled to think past the lust he roused in her. She clamped her thighs together and threw an arm over her hot face as she cursed him.

# CHAPTER 13

"Violet."

A rough shake jolted her awake. She opened her eyes and squinted at the figure beside her bed. "Jesse?"

"The paramedics are here."

She sat up and threw back the covers. "What? What happened?" she demanded and started toward the door.

He caught her arm. "They're putting Mom on the stretcher. Get dressed. We're following them to the hospital."

"What happened?" she shouted.

"Dad said she wasn't breathing right, so he called 911. Get dressed. I'll be in the living room."

He strode out of the room and closed the door behind him. She flew to her window and saw some neighbors standing on the front lawn as the ambulance pulled away. Even as panic seared her insides, she told herself Lynne was going to be fine. Just last night, they stayed up late playing Scrabble. She and Jesse had been pushing the boundaries on inappropriate words to make Lynne laugh. She glanced at the clock. It was almost two in the morning.

She splashed her face with water, brushed her teeth, and then pulled on jeans and a shirt before she rushed out of her room with her purse in hand. Jesse stood in front of the door leading to the garage. He pushed it open as she approached.

"Let's go," he said shortly.

"Dad's with her?" she asked urgently.

"Yeah."

She got in the passenger seat and buckled herself in. "What does that mean, she wasn't breathing right?"

"I don't know," he said as he backed out of the garage and turned a little too quickly, making the tires squeal as he sped down the empty road. "He said she was gasping for breath. He woke me up when the ambulance pulled up."

"Maybe she just needs an oxygen mask," she said as she twisted her hands together in her lap. When he barely tapped the brakes at a stop sign, she reached over and grabbed his arm. "Slow down, Jesse."

"I was calling her name, and she didn't respond," he said tightly.

Her fingers dug into his arm. "She's going to be okay. Just slow down. We don't want to get into an accident. We need to get to her in one piece."

It had been almost a week since their return from Florida. There was a steady stream of visitors to see Lynne. They didn't have to cook since everyone always brought a dish with them. Between cleaning, organizing her things, and caring for Lynne and her father, she was starting to feel a little ragged. Although Lynne tried to stay positive, there was no denying that she was deteriorating rapidly. Dad hovered over her night and day. She had to force him to rest when Lynne was occupied. Jesse ran interference with guests and showed them the door when Lynne pushed herself too hard. It had been a tense week, and it wasn't over yet.

She held on to Jesse's arm until he parked. They ran into the hospital and made their way to the emergency room, which was pandemonium. It took ten minutes to get answers to where Lynne had been taken. They ran into the room and were greeted by the sight of Dad kneeling beside the bed, face buried in the sheets.

"Dad?" she whispered.

When he raised his head, her legs went numb. He didn't need to say a word. It was written all over his face.

Jesse rounded the bed and took Lynne's hand. "What happened?"

"They said she had acute respiratory failure," Dad said in a lifeless voice. "She was declared dead on arrival."

"But she was fine a couple of hours ago," Violet whispered.

Dad shook his head. "I should have taken her to the hospital. I shouldn't have listened to her. She was always downplaying everything..."

When she put her arms around him, his shoulders began to shake as he broke down. Her mind disconnected from her body as she stared at Lynne, who looked as if she was sleeping. Her gaze went to Jesse, who stood on the opposite side of the bed. His eyes were glued to Lynne's face. He showed no emotion, but she saw his hand trembling as it held his mother's.

This couldn't be real life. She wasn't ready. Doctors came in. It took all of her will power to focus on what was being said. They were asking about what they wanted to do with Lynne's body, forms that needed to be signed, and other things that she couldn't hear over the buzzing in her ears. Neither she nor Dad was in any state to answer, so Jesse took over.

# CHAPTER 14

THE HOUSE WAS DEATHLY QUIET. SHE STARED AT THE CEILING AND watched the first hint of sunlight touch her bedroom curtains. It had been three days since Lynne passed. That wasn't enough time to wrap her mind around the fact that Mom was gone, but it *was* enough time to prepare a funeral. Everything was moving at supersonic speed. Mom's friends showed up at the hospital and took care of all the funeral arrangements, which had been planned months ago.

Two weeks ago, her biggest worry was how she was going to pay her bills. Now, she had moved back to Texas and was attending Lynne's funeral. Tears leaked out of the corner of her eyes. Life wasn't fair. Lynne should have had more time. How could she be here today and gone the next?

She, Dad, and Jesse were all handling Lynne's death in their own way. Dad had totally withdrawn. When she tried to check on him, he sent her away. She was too grief-stricken to fight him on it. Jesse seemed to be handling it the best. He dealt with the neighbors and family friends who stopped by to offer condolences. She hadn't seen him shed a tear.

She rolled out of bed and went into the bathroom. She took a shower and stared at her swollen eyes in the mirror. That wouldn't do. She walked out to the dark kitchen and put ice cubes in a towel and rested the cold compress over her eyes as she brewed coffee. After, she went into the back-yard to sit on the swing. It was an overcast day with light rain falling, a fitting atmosphere for the day ahead. Her eyes stung as the conversation she had with Lynne came back to her.

*Women are the glue that holds families together. I need you to promise me you'll keep the family intact.*

She had done a shit job so far. She took a steadying breath and sipped her coffee. If Lynne were here, she would tell her to dress in bright colors and put a smile on her face. She held the memory of Lynne laughing in the ocean in her mind as she went inside to get ready.

She dressed in a black long sleeve top and an ankle-length skirt with bright flowers on it. Her makeup was light and easily fixable, since she was sure she was going to bawl her eyes out.

She jumped when the door to Jesse's room opened. He was in his briefs and nothing else. He looked her over before he reached out and fingered her skirt.

"Mom would have liked this," he said.

She gave him a tremulous smile. "I know." Remembering her promise, she prompted, "Are you okay?"

"No."

He stripped off his underwear and stepped into the shower. She quickly exited and went to Dad's door. She knocked. Even though there was no answer, she opened the door and peeked in. Dad sat on the edge of the bed, dressed in his suit, staring at the wall.

"Dad?"

He didn't answer. She moved forward so she could see him properly. His face was completely blank, and his eyes were staring at something she couldn't see. He looked haggard and thinner than he had been a few days ago. She settled beside him and wrapped an arm around him.

"Are you okay?" she asked, voice warbling as she tried to suppress her emotions.

"No."

Honest and blunt, just like Jesse.

"I can make breakfast," she offered.

No response.

"Do you want coffee?"

Still nothing.

"Is there anything I can do?" she asked.

"No."

That hurt, but she tried not to take it personally. She gave him one last hug before she left the room and closed the door on her way out. She felt as if there was a bowling ball on her chest, restricting her airflow. It would be better once they laid Lynne to rest, right?

To keep herself busy, she made breakfast. She was just finishing up bacon and eggs when Jesse appeared in a dress shirt that matched his eyes and black slacks. He tossed his jacket over the back of a chair and stared out the window with his hands clasped behind him, his posture military straight.

She was setting the table when Dad appeared. He said nothing to either of them but grabbed the first set of keys he came across, which happened to be the ones for her Jeep.

"Dad?" she said tentatively.

"I want to clear my head before the funeral. I'll see you two there," Dad said without making eye contact.

"Isaac," Jesse began, but Dad held up a hand and slipped into the garage.

She stood in the kitchen, twisting her hands together, not sure whether she should do anything.

"He just needs space," Jesse said.

She held up a plate of food. "Come, eat."

They sat side by side at the table, neither of them eating much as it drizzled. The house seemed empty even with both of them there. She kept looking down the hallway, expecting Lynne to appear. When she felt the tears coming, she collected their plates and cleaned up the kitchen. All too soon, there was nothing left to do. Jesse had taken up his stance in front of the window again. She glanced at her phone and saw her messages piling up. She couldn't read the condolences. She had to conserve as much energy as possible for the funeral.

"Want to go for a drive?" he asked.

"Yes." She couldn't stay in this house that felt like an empty tomb. "Let me get my purse."

Dad took her car, which left the SUV. Jesse slid behind the driver's seat. The rain stopped as they left the house. The cloud cover gave them a break from the insufferable heat. She rested her head against the glass and tried to control her roiling emotions. Lynne was in a better place. That's all that mattered, right? She sighed heavily. Just because Lynne was no longer suffering didn't mean they wouldn't. What if Dad couldn't pull out of this? What would he do now that he didn't have Lynne to take care of? What was he going to do with the rest of his life now that he no longer had a partner by his side?

She rolled down the window as Jesse sped down the highway. Her hair was going to be a tangled mess, but she had a backup of everything in her purse and really...

nothing mattered anymore. Not her bills, not what her future held, or what people thought. All that mattered was the here and now. Life was so fucking short.

When he turned off the highway, she whipped her head around. "Jesse?"

"I need a moment."

"But..." Her voice died when she noticed he was sweating profusely, and his chest was moving rapidly beneath his shirt. "Are you okay?"

"I can't breathe."

He screeched to a stop in a small park, which was deserted this early in the morning. Before he put the car in park, he had his door open. He strode away, yanking on his tie. He stopped beneath a tree and braced his hand on the trunk as he bent over. She watched him for a moment before she slipped from the car and walked across the wet grass. She pressed against his back and wrapped her arms around him.

"I'm sorry," she whispered.

She held on tight as his body shook from the force of his grief. It was hard dealing with her own emotions but listening to him struggle to contain his sorrow hurt even more. She wasn't sure how long they stayed there, but she looked up when she felt the first fat drops of oncoming rain.

"Jesse, we have to get back in the car."

She stepped around to his front and saw that he was wearing the same glazed expression Dad had. She slipped an arm around his waist and led him back to the car. She pushed him into the passenger's seat before she ran around to the driver's side just as the heavens opened, and it began to pour. Jesse sat with his head tilted back and his eyes closed. He had undone the top buttons of his shirt, baring his throat. His tie hung loose around his neck.

When she reached for the keys, he grabbed her wrist. "Not yet."

"But..."

"Give me a minute."

She glanced at the clock and saw they had over an hour to kill. Rain tapped the windshield in an odd pattern. She was thankful for the rain guards, so she could crack the windows for air. She glanced at Jesse. A muscle flexed in his jaw as he fought to control his emotions. Even as she watched him, a tear slipped out of the corner of his eye.

Her heart clenched. "Jesse."

"I knew when I came home it would end like this," he said hoarsely. "I knew what to expect, but still..."

She stroked his cheek. "I know. I'm so sorry."

He leaned into her touch before he pressed his lips to her palm. "I wish I knew how much time we had left, so I knew how to live."

"What do you mean?"

His looked at her, revealing bloodshot blue orbs swirling with emotions too complex to define. Her eyes flooded with tears as she stared at him. He was in agony, and she couldn't stand it.

"You're gonna get through this," she said as the rain fell more heavily, hitting the roof of the car with significant force.

"Am I?" he asked as a tear slid down his cheek.

"You're the strongest man I know."

His damp eyes lit with an unholy light.

"I need you."

His voice was rough, almost angry.

"I'm here," she said unsteadily, unsure what he was asking for.

"I need you." His voice vibrated with meaning.

She felt a thunderbolt of panic. "I can't."

"Please."

He carried her hand to his crotch, which was tented. He forced her fingers to close around his cock.

"You can make it all go away. Help me."

Her mouth went dry. "Jesse."

"I need you so much I can't breathe," he said through clenched teeth.

She looked at the windshield, which had turned into a mini waterfall from the downpour, and then back at Jesse. Sweat dotted his forehead and chest. He was breathing heavily, as if he was wounded and couldn't breathe past the pain. She knew how he felt.

When her fingers moved to his zipper, he moved his hands away, so she could do what she needed to. She didn't let herself think. She leaned over the console as she pulled him out of his slacks. Her tongue swirled around his tip before she closed her mouth over him. His groan was loud enough to be heard over the rain and the distant crack of thunder. He stroked her hair as she worked him.

When he cursed, she lifted her head. "Jesse?"

His thumb moved over her wet lips. "I need more."

"What?"

He had the same lust-crazed expression he'd worn when she picked him up from the airport.

"I need your pussy. I need your arms around me, your legs squeezing me so tight I can't breathe. I need it all," he said as he gripped his dick and squeezed.

"But—"

He pressed his lips against hers. "Don't fight me," he pleaded as he kissed the corner of her mouth and then her cheek, ear, and chin. "Please, give me this. I'm not going to survive if—"

"Shh," she soothed and pushed against his chest. "Let me go in the back."

For a moment, he froze, and then he whispered a fervent, "Thank you."

She climbed over the console into the back. Most of the seats were still folded to accommodate their luggage when they came back from Florida. As she pulled her shirt over her head, Jesse awkwardly shimmied his way between the narrow opening and crawled toward her.

"Let me—" she began, but she didn't get to finish.

He swung her to the ground, lifted her skirt, and thrust inside her. She screamed, but the sound was cut off when his mouth crashed onto hers. He ground into her, sinking so deep, she fought back. He yanked on her hair and devoured her mouth savagely as he pumped feverishly until he climaxed. He threw back his head and roared, pounding his fist into the ground until he collapsed on top of her.

She swallowed hard as she stared up at the familiar car ceiling. Thunder rolled overhead while the rain came down in sheets, obliterating her vision of the forest around them and turned the trees into obscure, watercolor paintings.

Jesse groaned. "I'm sorry."

"Do you feel better?"

He shifted his head, so he could kiss her cheek. "No."

Her hand slid into his sweaty hair. "I'm sorry."

When he shifted his hips, she sucked in a breath.

"I don't think I can feel okay today, but now I can breathe," he said against her ear. "Thank you."

"We should—"

He grabbed her face and turned it toward him. His lips covered hers and when she opened her mouth to protest, his tongue interrupted. Thoughts of the funeral slipped away as he paid homage—sucking on her nipples until she sobbed and fucking her so slowly that she almost ripped his shirt as she urged him on. No matter what demands she made or what she did to him, he kept his pace slow, almost reverent, and nudged her into a climax that made her shudder as if she were having a seizure.

He brushed back her tangled hair. "I love you."

She tensed beneath him.

"I'll keep saying it until you believe me," he said.

"We should go."

He made no move to get off her. On the contrary, he began to rock against her. He was hard again and clearly not going anywhere until he came. His eyes searched hers with such naked emotion that she looked away. He pressed his lips against her cheek.

"You can't hide from me, Violet."

"Hurry, we have to go!" she snapped.

He ground her against the hard floor. She punched his shoulder.

"Jesse!"

"You can choose a different path for us. You can forgive me and love me, but you reject me instead. Anything you ask of me, I'd give. You're all I want."

"I can't do this!"

"You have to," he hissed before he lifted her thighs and stabbed as deep as he could and spilled in her womb.

He pressed his forehead against hers as he tried to catch his breath.

"You know what hurts worse than laying my mother to rest today?"

Her breath stalled.

"Knowing that the one person I love more than her is still here and doesn't want to be with me."

He pressed a gentle kiss to her lips before he rolled off

her. Violet lay there for a full minute as she tried to manage the pain. Minutes passed. She listened to the sound of his harsh breathing steady before she reached for her bag filled with everything she needed to make herself presentable again.

She felt his eyes on her as she redid her makeup, smoothed her hair, and cleaned herself with baby wipes and a pack of Kleenex. She didn't meet his eyes as she tended to him as well, brushing back his tangled hair and wiping away smears of lipstick.

When she tried to move away, he grabbed hold of her. "You can't forgive me?"

"We need to go," she said in a monotone.

"Violet."

She turned her face away as her eyes burned with tears. "I can't do this today, Jesse."

When she pushed, his hand dropped away. She nabbed her shirt as she crawled back into the passenger seat and slipped it on. Jesse followed and retook his spot behind the wheel. She closed her eyes as he left the park and headed to church. The short drive seemed to take an eternity. When they pulled up, she saw several cars in front, including her Jeep.

Jesse reached for his jacket and shrugged it on before he grabbed an umbrella and came around to her side. She gripped his arm as her heels sank into the soggy grass.

They walked into the church and were greeted by the funeral organizers and close friends who had arrived early to see if they could help with anything. She made small talk for a few minutes before she walked over to her father, who stood in front of the stage. There was a riot of flowers everywhere, along with a photo of mom and a collage of images from her life.

"Hey," she said.

Dad didn't acknowledge her. She wrapped an arm around his waist and squeezed.

"Dad?"

He pulled away and walked out the back of the church. Her heart thudded in her ears as he stood on the small landing, hands clasped behind his back as he stared out at the rain.

A hand squeezed her shoulder. "Don't take it personally," Pastor Sonny said.

She brushed away a tear and tried to cover up her hurt with a smile. "Right."

"He's grieving. Everyone reacts differently. I'm working with him." Pastor Sonny chucked her under the chin, something he used to do when she was a little girl. "It's good to see you, Violet. Jesse, too. I hope to see you in church in the future."

She made a noncommittal noise. As someone called his name and he moved away, she knew there was no way in hell she would step foot in this building again unless there was a wedding or funeral. She looked down the aisle and saw Jesse watching her from the opposite end. She turned away and tried to rein in her emotions. She wanted to be anywhere but here.

Too soon, people began to arrive. She and Jesse took their posts near the stage to greet everyone and accept condolences. She was very aware of her father's absence. Some of his friends went to talk to him, but no one could bring him inside. She glanced at Jesse. The tears and vulnerability he displayed earlier had disappeared. She had never felt so alone.

Pastor Sonny managed to coax Dad inside for the service. She sat between Dad and Jesse in the front row and stared straight ahead with her hands fisted on her lap. The service was mercifully short. She could barely hear the pastor over the sound of thunder cracking overhead. Neither she nor Dad got up to speak, but Jesse did. He quoted one of Lynne's favorite scriptures and spoke fondly of the woman who had made him into the man he was today. He made everyone laugh through the tears.

When the service was over, she turned to Dad. "Can I ride with you to the wake?"

He walked away as if he hadn't heard her. She watched as he strode through the rain, slid into her Jeep, and drove off without saying a word to anyone. Several people cast her sympathetic looks and patted her on the back.

"Let's go," Jesse said.

Neither of them said a word during the drive to Lynne's friend's house. The wake wasn't as bad as she thought it was going to be. It was relaxed and casual. They ate and lounged around while telling stories about Lynne. Everyone wanted to know what her plans were now that she had moved back. She had no answers and said she was going to take it a day at a time.

Dad showed his face at the wake only long enough not to be rude before he disappeared again. Jesse followed him outside and leaned on his window and spoke to him before he came back inside. When she caught his eye, he shrugged, indicating he wasn't worried.

When they pulled up to the house that evening, the Jeep was missing. She rubbed her aching temples.

"Should I call him?" she asked Jesse in a voice hoarse from crying.

"He'll be fine. He just needs to be alone."

She walked into the house and looked up at Jesse. His face was pale and drawn.

"Are you going to be okay?"

Moody eyes moved over her. "Eventually."

The darkness threatening to erupt from him made her stomach flutter. She stepped back and made her way to her bedroom. She locked her doors before she fell face first on the bed and bawled her eyes out.

# CHAPTER 15

She stared at the mess she had made of her room and threw her hands in the air. It had been three days since the funeral. To keep herself busy, she unpacked, which had turned her room into a disaster area. Without Reese's organizing skills, she had somehow barricaded her closet and bathroom door shut and couldn't even make it to the bed without stepping over piles of crap. There were boxes everywhere and belongings she had no place for. She kicked a pile of clothes before she walked out. She felt as if she was coming out of her skin.

She peeked in her parent's bedroom even though she knew what she would find. Dad wasn't there, of course. He left every morning before she and Jesse woke and didn't come home until they were asleep. She was alarmed, but Jesse wasn't, so she wouldn't call for an intervention just yet. She knew losing Lynne would devastate her father and had been prepared for many things, but his flat refusal to communicate and his icy coldness wasn't one of them. She moved home to be here for him during this time, and he deserted her. She felt as if she lost both parents. She thought they would deal with this together, but Dad made it clear he wanted to be alone, leaving her with no one to turn to.

She glanced into Jesse's bedroom, which was also empty. She felt a spark of relief when she found him sitting on the couch in the living room. He sat with his hands folded in his lap, eyes closed, and head tipped back. She knew he wasn't sleeping. He was trying to escape in his head, but it wasn't working. Grief radiated from him. If Dad was here, she could focus on him, but he wasn't, so Jesse would have to do. Against her better judgment, she started forward.

"Can I get you anything?" she asked.

He opened bloodshot eyes and stared at her for a beat before he shook his head. He said little since the funeral, but he was always around. She had a feeling if she wasn't here, he would be out of the house like Dad. If she had any close friends here, she might be with them, but she hadn't reconnected with anyone enough to barf her feelings on them. So, she was stuck in the house with pent-up energy and her emotions tearing her in every direction.

She settled on the opposite end of the couch and stared blindly at the blank TV. She felt so damn lost. Crying didn't help. Keeping busy didn't work either. She slept little in the past few days and couldn't remember the last thing she ate. She wished Dad would stop avoiding her. She needed him more than ever.

"Violet."

She whipped her head toward Jesse and saw he was watching her. He lifted his arm in an unspoken invitation. She didn't hesitate. She dove at him, burying her face in his chest, and burst into tears. She cried so hard; she couldn't catch her breath. His arms came around her, giving her the hug she craved, the comfort she felt she would perish without.

"Shh, it's okay," he said as he stroked her hair.

"I m-miss her s-so much," she stammered.

"I know. Me too."

"I-I don't know what to do, and Dad... I don't know how to help him."

"Let him be, Vi."

"But he shouldn't—"

"He'll work it out on his own."

She sniffled. "How do you know?"

"Because I'm a man."

"So?"

"Men react to pain in two ways. We run or we fight. Don't get in his face. You won't like the reaction you get. Let him deal with it on his own."

"But you're here," she pointed out.

"I'm here in case you want to fight," he said.

Her lip curved in a sad smile before her face crumpled. She slumped against him. She should keep her guard up, but she needed touch more than anything in the world. She didn't know how to feel about Jesse. At times, he was her adversary, ally, lover, worst enemy, and protector. Currently, he was offering her a safe place, so she would take what he was willing to give. She didn't want to be alone right now.

She rested her cheek against his chest and listened to his steady heartbeat. Her mind swung from her worries about Dad and Jesse to seeking employment to changing her car registration and everything in between. She was spiraling. She had so many things to do, but she couldn't choose which task to do first, so she did nothing.

Jesse stroked her back. "I have to leave soon."

Panic ripped through her. She looked up, unaware her hand twisted in his shirt. "Leave?"

"I have to report for duty in Japan. I've already made my flights."

She felt as if she was going to shatter. "When?"

"I have a little over a week left here."

She leapt to her feet and faced him with her hands fisted at her sides. "You're only telling me this now?"

"You knew I'd have to leave."

"Not so soon!" she shouted and stomped her foot. "You can't go. You owe me!"

"I do?"

"Yes, you do!" she bellowed as she paced in a circle. "You changed me and then waltzed out of my life to play the honorable soldier serving his country and left me in shambles."

"You wanted me to leave."

"And now I'm telling you to stay, so what are you going to do?" she challenged.

He shook his head. "I have orders."

"Screw your orders! I need you!" She flung her arms wide. "I can't do this by myself!"

"You'll get through it."

"Don't go!"

His brows drew together. "Violet."

"You can't leave me like this!"

He grabbed her hand and drew her between his thighs. "You know I'd do almost anything for you, but I can't."

"But..." Tears slipped down her cheeks. "I'm going to be all alone."

He tugged her onto his lap, so she was straddling him. "I'll come back."

She shook her head. "You won't."

He clasped her face and brushed away her tears with his thumb. "Are you going to keep the promise you made me on the beach?"

*Promise you won't cut me out of your life again.*

She nodded.

"Then I'll be back." He gave her a bittersweet smile as he stroked her cheek. "Even though I want to rip my heart out because it hurts so much, just looking at you makes me feel better. You've always been my morphine."

He tipped her against him, so he could rest his face in the hollow of her throat. He let out a long breath as his hands ran up her sides. Slowly, he relaxed, as if her proximity calmed him.

"You and Isaac are all I have left," he said hoarsely. "I need you in my life."

"I'm not going anywhere," she said as she wrapped her arms around him.

"Fuck, Violet, I'm desperate for you."

She couldn't resist the forlorn plea in his tone. She grabbed a handful of his hair and yanked, so his head tipped up. She planted her lips on his and sank deep. Lust swiped its claws across her belly. She answered the call. The same madness that came over her on the beach welled up inside of her again. She wasn't concerned about right or wrong. All she cared about was numbing the pain.

She kept her mouth on his as she shifted back so she could reach down and grip him through his silky basketball shorts. He made a wheezing sound and gripped her hip as she stroked. She wanted to make him feel good and forget what they had lost and was still trickling through their fingers. His mouth hardened beneath hers. She shifted back on his iron thighs to pull him out of his shorts.

"Violet," he panted.

She slipped off his lap to whip her shirt over her head and shuck her jeans. He pumped his hand on his cock as he watched her. When she was naked, she resumed her position on his lap and held him so she could impale herself on him.

Veins stood out on his neck as he gritted, "You're killing me."

The delicious stretch of being invaded is just what she needed. She was barely wet enough to take him, so she rocked until he was balls deep in her. She needed this more than she needed to eat, more than she needed to breathe. This would make everything better and chase away her doubts and fear. Nothing mattered but this.

She clutched the back of the couch as she moved on him. She rode him the way she had always wanted to. Greedy, forceful, rough—the way she couldn't be with other men. He was her willing slave. The way he stared at her spurred her on.

"Take me," he groaned and dropped his head back and swore. "Who the fuck taught you that?"

"You," she panted in his ear and nipped.

He gripped her hair and twisted to keep her still for biting kisses. "Love me."

He began to move with her, thrusting up as she bore down.

"You want me, Violet?"

She moved faster, plastering her bare chest against his shirt as she raced to the finish line. "Give me what I need!"

"Ask nicely."

"Fuck you! You owe me!"

"I'll give you whatever you want if you tell me what I want to hear."

She glared at him. "Never."

He smiled and slammed up, nearly unseating her. "We'll see about that."

"What the hell is going on here?"

Her father's voice cut through the passionate haze more effectively than if God himself had materialized in their living room. They froze. All that beautiful lust vanished in a nanosecond. Her mind went blank with horror. Her father couldn't be here while she was naked as the day she was born, and Jesse was inside her. This had to be a nightmare.

Jesse's gaze was fixed over her shoulder. He had a strange look on his face. She couldn't move without revealing more than she already was. She was forced to stay impaled on Jesse's lap with her back to her father.

"How long has this been going on?" Dad asked.

She began to shake. Jesse reached for a quilt draped over the back of the couch and swung it around her to cover her body.

"I asked you two a question."

Oh, God. She took the coward's way out and buried her face in Jesse's shoulder. He kissed her temple and shifted her as he sat upright. He didn't seem perturbed that Dad just caught them mid-fuck. How was he still hard and pulsing inside of her?

"We've been doing this since we were in high school," Jesse said.

She jerked and would have raised her head, but the grip on her nape kept her face tucked against him. What the hell was he *doing*? He was telling the truth? Her father would kill him!

"High school."

Her father's flat tone made her shudder.

"Yes, sir," Jesse said.

"Why did you hide it?"

"We didn't think you'd approve."

Again, she tried to straighten, but Jesse kept her pinned against him.

"And you think this is better? Sneaking around all this time?"

"It's the only thing we could do," Jesse said.

"Why has she been avoiding you all these years?"

"She was mad I enlisted in the military."

This time, she managed to break his hold. She straightened and braced her hands on his chest. Her throat was bone dry, but she couldn't let him tell these lies. Jesse stared at her, as calm as could be. What the hell was wrong with him?

"Is this true, Vi?" Dad asked.

She stared at Jesse, silently willing him to tell the truth.

Jesse cupped her cheek. "Answer him, baby."

Baby? She wasn't his baby. Why was he acting like they dated? They didn't date, they just had sex—a *lot* of it.

Jesse's eyes went over her shoulder. "She's in shock. We never wanted you to find out like this."

"Did you ever want me to find out?"

Dad's disapproval was like imaginary smoke, cloying the air and making it hard to breathe.

"I wanted to tell you, but Violet didn't feel the same way."

"You're gonna do right by my daughter," Dad said.

As his words penetrated, she shoved off Jesse and fell on her ass. She clasped the quilt to her chest as she turned to find her father walking toward the front door.

"Dad!"

He turned his head as she got to her feet and immediately averted his gaze.

"This isn't what it seems," she said desperately.

Jesse gripped her shoulder. She shrugged him off and took a step toward her father, who refocused on her. His eyes were dull and lifeless. She wasn't sure if it was from grief or shock. All she knew was he had never looked at her like that before.

"I raised you better," he whispered.

She felt as if he plunged a knife in her stomach. She hunched over as pain seared her insides. She reached for him in supplication, her need to wipe that look from his face paramount, but he took a step back and shook his head.

"I can't look at you right now."

"Let me explain…"

"I won't let you become your mother," he said, voice shaking with emotion. "I don't believe in sex before marriage and since you two have been carrying on since high school, you're going to make this right. You two made your bed. Now you're going to lie in it."

"But Dad—"

He walked through the front door. When she tried to go after him, Jesse wrapped his arms around her. When she opened her mouth to call out to him, Jesse clamped a hand over her lips. She caught a glimpse of her dad walking to the SUV parked in the driveway. Why hadn't he parked in the garage? If he had, they would have had time to disengage and avoid this disaster.

Even as she struggled to comprehend what happened, Jesse lifted her off her feet. He ignored her muffled scream and carried her down the hall to his room and tossed her on the bed. He pounced on her before she could roll away and pinned her arms over her head as she raged.

"I hate you!" she shouted as tears streamed down her face.

"Did you hear what he said?"

"You screwed up everything!"

He released her wrist to cup her cheek. "It's done, baby."

She slammed her fist into his chest. "It's *not* done! He can't order me to do anything! This is a free country!"

"He wants what's best for you."

"You aren't what's best for me! You're a nightmare!"

"A nightmare you crave. Do you want to get disowned?"

She bared her teeth. "I'm not marrying you!"

"Dad just gave us his blessing."

"Because he thinks I'm a whore! He—he thinks I'm like my mother..." She turned her face to the side as she let out a sob.

"It's gonna be okay."

"It'll never be okay. I haven't been okay since you. You ruined me!"

He sat up and whipped off his shirt. When she tried to get away, he sat on her stomach and hooked his thumb in the waistband of his shorts.

"You think I'm going to let you touch me? You're out of your mind!" she shrieked as she clawed his thighs.

"I'm going to do more than touch you," he promised as he yanked his shorts off and made a space for himself between her thighs. He closed his eyes as he slid inside her, deaf to her struggles and verbal abuse. He moaned as he pressed his forehead against hers.

"I love you, Violet."

"You lied to him!" she wailed.

"I told him my truth." He stroked her cheek. "The truth you refuse to accept. You didn't want me not to leave. Now you can come with me."

"*What?*"

"We can see the world. I'll give you whatever you want."

"This will never work," she moaned.

"It will. It *is*. Don't you feel it?"

"I'm not talking about sex!" she shouted.

"Sex is how our souls speak to one another," he crooned. "No one will take better care of you than me."

She stared at him as he braced himself over her. He was flushed with desire, eyes sparkling with excitement as he ground against her. She bared her teeth and sank her nails into his back. He grinned as she drew blood.

"You want to punish me, baby?" he breathed. "Do your worst. I can take it. I can take anything now that I have you."

"I hate you!"

"I love you," he said fervently as he covered her face with kisses. "I always have. I can make you happy. We can start fresh. I'll take care of everything."

"I can't," she began and hissed when he planted himself deep.

"You will," he countered. "Dad won't let you stay here, not when he knows we've been having an affair since we were teenagers."

"I didn't..." she began hotly but was interrupted when he flipped her onto her front and slammed into her from behind. She screamed into his sheets.

"I can fuck you into forgetting that you hate me," he panted in her hair. "Whoever you need me to be, I'll be. Say you'll have me."

She buried her face in the mattress as he fucked her, balls smacking her ass as he thrust. Her body was buzzing. Ecstasy was within her grasp. A hand gripped her throat and squeezed.

"Say yes," he hissed.

She clenched her teeth as pleasure nipped at her heels.

"Fucking say it!" he roared.

"Yes," she gasped as her climax ripped through her. She moaned like a bitch in heat and screamed his name as he fucked her raw.

When she lay exhausted and limp beneath him, he brushed her hair away from her face and rested his cheek against hers.

"You won't regret this," he vowed.

# AUTHOR'S NOTE

Thank you for giving this story a chance! I wrote a bonus scene of Jesse's arrival in Austin from his point of view. To read it, join my newsletter: https://www.subscribepage.com/CIbonus.

I do intend to write a sequel, but I am currently under contract for several projects as dark romance author, Mia Knight. When I have a block of time to continue the *Possessing Violet Series*, I will update my blog and social media! I'm not sure if Violet and Jesse will have one or two more books. I have some wild ideas for the continuation. We'll see how many installments it takes to wrap up their story.

You can sign up to my newsletter to stay informed about future releases. If you can, please leave a review, they help me out so much!

Sincerely,

Dinah

# BOOKS BY DINAH HARPER

**Possessing Violet Series:**

Corrupt Obsession

Corrupt Idol

# About the Author

Dinah Harper will have you squirming in your seat and looking around to make sure no one can see what you're reading. The *Possessing Violet Series* is the first of many erotic novels she has planned.

Please be patient. She is currently under contract for several projects as dark romance author, Mia Knight. When she resumes her work as Dinah Harper, she will update her blog and social media. Sign up to her newsletter (https://www.subscribepage.com/DinahHarperNews) to stay informed about future releases!

Website: https://dinahharper.com

instagram.com/authordinahharper

bookbub.com/authors/dinah-harper

goodreads.com/dinahharper

reamstories.com/miaknightwrites